We Love Harry Potter!

We Love Harry Potter!

We'll Tell You Why

SHARON MOORE

St. Martin's Griffin ☙ New York

Design by Lisa Pifher

ISBN 0-312-26481-x

First St. Martin's Griffin Edition: December 1999

10 9 8 7 6 5 4 3 2 1

To David W. Moore
and
Royall T. Moore

Contents

Introduction 1
WHAT MAKES THE HARRY POTTER BOOKS SPECIAL

About J. K. Rowling 4
AUTHOR OF THE HARRY POTTER BOOKS

1. Our Comments About the Harry Potter Books 6
WHY AND WHAT WE LOVE ABOUT THE BOOKS

2. Dear Harry . . . 68
LETTERS WE HAVE WRITTEN IN SCHOOL

3. What Wizards Eat 78
RECIPES AND COMMENTS ABOUT
THE FOOD IN THE BOOKS

4. How We Play Quidditch 87
OUR GROUND RULES AND METHODS
OF PLAYING THE GAME

5. What Grown-Ups Say
About the Harry Potter Books 96
WHY AND WHAT PARENTS, GRANDPARENTS, TEACHERS
AND BOOKSELLERS LOVE ABOUT THE BOOKS

6. Trivia Quiz 104
TEST YOUR KNOWLEDGE ABOUT THE HARRY POTTER BOOKS

7. Survey of Our Opinions 107
WHO AND WHAT ARE OUR FAVORITES;
WHO AND WHAT WE LIKE LEAST

8. Word Wizardry 108
BREAK THE MAGICIAN'S SPELL AND FIGURE OUT
THESE WIZARD WORDS

9. Wonderful Ways to Be a Wizard 111

10. What We Think Harry Potter's
Parents Were Like 114
A SUMMARY OF OUR THEORIES ABOUT THEIR
OCCUPATIONS, RESIDENCES AND RELATIONSHIPS

11. What We'd Like to See in the Future Books
About Harry Potter 116

We Love Harry Potter!

Introduction

WHAT MAKES THE HARRY POTTER BOOKS SPECIAL

It's not hard to understand why we love the Harry Potter books. The first few paragraphs of the first one, *Harry Potter and the Sorcerer's Stone*, make you feel so excited, amused and annoyed that you want to turn the page and keep going. You've just got to find out how really awful the Dursleys are!

The Harry Potter books are different from other children's fantasy books because they happen in the modern day. Their main character, Harry, is an ordinary kid who grows up in an ordinary (if dreadful) suburban family, and not in a fairy-tale land. So readers can identify with him as a real kid before he leads us off into the wonderful world of wizardry. And no matter what happens—how scary, how mysterious, how dangerous—we feel safe because we're with Harry.

Years ago, kids who played Dungeons and Dragons belonged to a sort of unofficial club, and only they understood the rules or knew the names. The same is true of Harry Potter fans—we love to collect and talk about trivia from the books, such as names of characters, places, activities and events. Which seems perfectly natural, since we spend a lot of time learning facts and figures in school!

The names of people and places in the Harry Potter books are part of the fun. There are lots of silly-sounding *gr*'s and *duh*'s: Grunnings, Gringotts, Gryffindor; Dudley, Dursley and Dumbledore. There are sneaky-sounding *s*'s: Slytherins, Snape, Severus, Sirius and Scabbers. The *h*'s are kind of heroic: Hogwarts, Hedwig, Hermione and Hagrid. The *f*'s are often unpleasant types: Filch and Flitwick. Then there are just funny-sounding names like Peeves, and Weasley. The names that sound French are usually difficult people: Madam Pince, Madam Pomfrey, and Malfoy.

Then there's the name of the game, Quidditch, which sounds like a combination of the three kinds of balls used: the Quaffle, the Bludgers, and the Golden Snitch.

And the passwords into the Gryffindor common room are always strange: "pig snout," "Capu Draconis," "scurvy cur," "oddsbodkins," and "wattlebird." It's as if the words themselves have magic powers—just look how afraid everyone is of saying the real name of You-Know-Who!

Some words are just plain tricky, like the name of the Mirror of Erised, which is "desire" spelled backwards—as it would be when seen in a mirror!

It's hard to say what we like most about these books. There are scary adventures, magic and funny things that happen, but there are also classes and homework and parents, so that makes it almost like real life. Children don't ordinarily have much to say about what's going to happen to them, but Harry and his friends can use the magic to make things go the way they want them to. Don't we all wish we had such magical powers?

—*Sharon Moore*

About J. K. Rowling

AUTHOR OF THE HARRY POTTER BOOKS

J. K. Rowling grew up in a working-class family in Edinburgh, Scotland. She had always made up stories, and wrote her first book, *Rabbit*, when she was six. After she grew up, she graduated from Exeter University, became a teacher, got married and had a baby.

Then came a time she calls "a bad patch" in her life when she was out of work, divorced and so poor that she went on welfare (or "the dole," as it is called in Britain). She and her baby lived in an apartment without any heat, so sometimes she went to a café to keep warm. There, she began scribbling ideas for stories about Harry Potter on napkins. Later, she began writing the first book, and was helped by a grant from the Scottish Arts Council. She sent her manuscript to many publishers and literary agents before she found a buyer. Soon the book, which was published in England under the title *Harry Potter and the Philosopher's Stone*, became a bestseller in England and America.

J. K. Rowling says that, right from the start, she planned to write seven Harry Potter books, one for each year he goes to Hogwarts School of Witchcraft and Wizardry. In fact, as she said on the Rosie O'Donnell TV show (October 14, 1999), she has already written the last chapter of book number seven (although she hasn't finished book number four yet).

She is slender, blond and friendly, with a dry sense of humor. She likes to be called "Jo," which is short for Joanne. Since the books were published under the name "J. K. Rowling," some of her friends have nicknamed her "Jake," which she doesn't like very much.

She sometimes gets annoyed when people mention her "bad patch," because it doesn't represent her whole life. She is still very surprised, even astonished, at the success of her books, because she says it's very unusual for anyone to write a bestseller, and she claims she is lucky to have done so. She can remember what it was like to be a school-age child, and imagines herself back there when she is writing the Harry Potter books.

Jo Rowling has said that in future books, Harry continues to grow up, so readers should not be surprised when he begins to notice girls. Also, she says, there may be more serious evil in the books to come.

1

Our Comments About the Harry Potter Books

WHY AND WHAT WE LOVE ABOUT THE BOOKS

Carolyn Singer Minott,* 10 years old

I get so involved reading the Harry Potter books that I feel like I'm inside Harry's world.

If I went to wizard school I'd study everything: spells and counterspells, Defense Against the Dark Arts—but not Potions, because I don't like Snape. He only saved Harry because he was in debt to Harry, and so just evened the score.

I love how Hermione gets into stuff, like the Polyjuice Potion. She's a very smart girl, although sometimes she overdoes it. Sometime she's a pain in the neck and I get pretty mad at her.

Dumbledore is very fair. He hasn't expelled Harry or his friends because of the trouble they get into. Snape is mean but he makes the book more interesting. The Dursleys aren't believable, but you need something to hate, so Go, Harry! Dudley looks like a big fat balloon with a fat face and blond hair. I loved it when Hagrid gave Dudley a tail!

Buckbeak the hippogriff was wonderful, especially when he injured Malfoy. Hippogriffs are very sweet but they can be dangerous. I love their pride. I loved the way the two fugitives, Buckbeak and Sirius Black, escaped together at the end of the third book.

The wizard crackers at the Christmas feast were great. I loved the way the pictures moved, and also when the knight Sir Cadogan defended the entrance to Gryffindor after the fat lady's picture was slashed by Sirius Black. It was comical when Ron says "shut up!" to the picture. The ghosts and the pixies were funny, too.

It was neat how some wizards could turn themselves into animals—they were called animages. They could go anywhere and listen to what they weren't supposed to. I'd turn myself into a poisonous frog, or a cat.

I didn't like Madam Trelawney. Madam Pomfrey's too protective. She lives in her own little world. That's not my cup of tea. But I loved how the antidote to spells was chocolate.

Gilderoy Lockhart has a big head and a little brain. He thought of himself as the greatest, but he didn't equal one Harry. He wasn't very smart.

Moaning Myrtle was a pest. She just wanted attention.

I liked Lupin. His name fits him (he was a werewolf). I was unhappy to see him go.

I'd like to see what happens to the first-year students in the future. Colin Creevey was a clinging vine but it would be interesting to see what he turns into. I admired Cho Chang (the Ravenclaw Seeker). I hope we see her again.

If someone is going to be killed, I don't want it to be Ginny. I'd like to see Ginny and Hermione hook up. I'd like to see Percy leave, though; he was a party pooper, too full of himself, and his head's as big as Lockhart's. I'd like to see Snape get the job of Defense Against the Dark Arts Professor; it may take out some of the tension. I don't think Snape is involved in the Dark Arts, he's just unpleasant. He treats everyone except Slytherins badly.

I was glad Mrs. Norris got petrified.

I like the way they use different languages, like Latin and French.

I'd love to play Quidditch—I'd love to fly a broomstick. I'd catch the ball and rub it into a Slytherin's face.

Some children have trouble imagining or remembering what Dudley Dursley looks like. It's often hard for children to picture a character unless he or she looks like someone they know, especially if the chracter is a strange-looking person. And there are some very strange-looking people in fiction! But the fun part of reading is making up your own image of a book character's appearance.

*See the Quidditch chapter for Carolyn's comments about playing the game.

Carter Brown Grotta,* 6 years old

It was cool that Harry didn't know he was a witch at first.

We play Harry Potter on the playground at school. I bring the Harry Potter books and another book that I call Tom Riddle's diary. My friend Nicky Silvi is Harry Potter, and I play Ron.

What we need to do is make a map of the playground because all of the other kids who have forts there are always attacking us, especially the girls' forts. So we are making a map of our Harry Potter land, although we don't know what we're going to call it yet.

We're also making a map of Hogwarts. We need to have a place to keep our books, journals, secrets, Quidditch balls and stuff.

One thing is pretty bad. We don't have enough people. We only have eight, and we need 18 more— that's how many people there were in Hogwarts.

I made a broomstick out of sticks, and tied a lot of threads together for the broom part. I have a sticker that looks like a lightning bolt that I stick on my forehead. Then I look like Harry Potter, because I wear glasses, too.

I made a wand out of a bunch of sticks connected with a rubber band. I put red-colored paper around it, so I have a red wand.

I made the Tom Riddle diary up especially. I'm trying to get some red blobs (like the ink Harry spilled on the diary) to put on it.

*See the Quidditch chapter for Carter's comments about playing the game.

★ ★ ★

Emily Lebowitz, * 14 years old

The Harry Potter books take you to another reality, to a place that's out of this world—a place you'd never think of by yourself.

I'd like to go to wizard school, but I'm not sure which house I'd want to be in. Probably Harry's. I'd study potions and spells, and create things like food, or medicine—things you might not be able to make with what we have in our world, like a cure for cancer.

I love Quidditch. If I could play I'd like to be a Seeker. I'd love to fly on a broomstick, and see the world from an aerial point of view. It would be easier than waiting until I'm old enough to have a car!

What's great about Harry is that, after all the abuse he puts up with from the Dursleys, who put

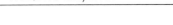

him in the cupboard and everything, he still has a positive outlook on life.

Hermione is a doer. She always tries to do everything, even though she doesn't always succeed.

I'd like to have Every Flavor Beans that taste like strawberry, or other real fruit, like pears, or Coke, or corn muffins, or Thanksgiving dinner—you could have a whole set that tastes like turkey, cranberry sauce and stuffing. I'd hate to get liver, or tongue.

I didn't care for the Chocolate Frogs, because I have a pet frog. Her name is Cher. I keep her in a cage and feed her crickets.

In the next books, I hope something bad happens to the Dursleys; for example, Uncle Vernon loses his job. They should get a taste of what they're doing to Harry. They should have to treat Harry as an equal for a change.

I think Sirius Black and Harry may be related. Black is a good guy, really looking out for Harry's well-being in some way. But I'm not sorry Harry didn't go to live with him. It would change everything if Harry wasn't at Hogwarts. It's harder for him to live there, but the tension adds to the excitement of the book.

I want to see what happens to Harry after all his adventures. I know there are supposed to be seven books, but I'd like to see an eighth, a conclusion book. I want to see what happens after Hogwarts, what Harry becomes, where he lives and what he does.

*See the Quidditch chapter for Emily's comments about playing the game.

Ariel Doctoroff,* 9 years old

My sister Jenna is too young to read the books, but she's grateful for Harry Potter because I tell her all about him.

The books are exciting, and so is the magic.

I like the funny names of people and places.

Harry is my favorite character, but I also like Ron and Hermione and of course I don't like Snape and Malfoy.

My favorite animal is the hippogriff. They're funny. They look something like an ostrich.

I like being scared. I liked the dementors because they were so scary. My favorite scary part is the end of the Chamber of Secrets, with the snake sliding around, and Tom Riddle is really Voldemort and Ginny is trapped in the chamber, about to die—but then she gets saved.

The hippogriffs are half-horse, half-eagle, so they would indeed look something like an ostrich.

*See the Quidditch chapter for Ariel's comments about playing the game.

Phillip Zelonky, 9 years old

The books are interesting, not boring like a lot of books.

The Quidditch game is my favorite thing about the books. I like the chess games, too.

My favorite characters were Sirius Black and Snape, because they're exciting. But I think they should have done more evil things—if they were more bad, the story would be more exciting.

I didn't like Madam Pooch,* or the Dursleys.

I'd like to be able to make up a spell. It would be really neat to use a spell to do something like turn on the TV!

I heard all about the fourth book already—my friend heard about it on the Internet.

*Madam Hooch was the Gryffindor Quidditch team's coach, and not a bad sort of person. It's possible Phillip means Madam Pomfrey, the head of the hospital wing, who was always hustling away visitors. Many of J. K. Rowling's characters' names sound partly French and partly English.

Josie Chen, 12 years old

The books are full of mystery and fast adventures. It's especially good when Harry is sneaking up on somebody like Quirrell or being chased by Malfoy in a Quidditch game.

I want to have a dragon for a pet. They don't have to be as big as the one Hagrid was trying to raise, Norbert. They can be little and cute.

I tried to solve the problem with the seven bottles in the first book, and I got most of it, I think. But I'm glad I didn't have to be the one to drink them because I might've got it wrong, and then I'd get poisoned.

My guess is that Harry's parents went back to the Muggle world, took regular jobs and did magic stuff in secret, like spells and potions that made their Muggle jobs easier. Like, maybe they put a spell on money stocks so they'd make more money.

I heard that Harry gets a girlfriend in the next book. I hope it's Cho Chang, the Seeker for the Ravenclaw team. She's pretty and has almost the same name as me.

Children are natural problem-solvers and they love puzzles, riddles and word games. There are plenty of these in the Harry Potter books, which is one of the reasons why children love them. The mysterious power of words is an important element in magic through the ages, and the ability to understand foreign languages and codes was a basic skill that all wizards and witches had to know.

Becky Rubin, 10 years old

The beginning is cool, when Harry goes off to Hogwarts—how he runs through Barrier Nine and Three-Quarters, and Dumbledore makes the plates fill up with food.

My favorite character is Hermione, because she's funny and so perfect, always trying to get Harry and Ron to do their homework. Percy is funny, too. I like the Weasleys.

Hermione is very brave. I picture her as tall and skinny with brownish red hair and brown eyes.

I didn't figure out the puzzles, but Hermione did. She's a total Einstein. The chess game at the end of the first book was exciting and scary.

I like the way the books leave you things to imagine and figure out.

My favorite animal is Hedwig, Harry's owl. It's cool to have an owl deliver a letter and get a return.

I'd like most Every Flavor Beans, especially chocolate, but I'd hate to get a pepper one.

Malfoy and his father and You-Know-Who were the characters I didn't like. Snape wasn't as bad as Filch, but Snape was a bully.

You hear more about Harry's father than his mother because his father was killed fighting You-Know-Who. His father was fighting because men are more brave. Harry's mother just tried to protect him, because women love kids.

I think Harry's father probably worked for the

Ministry of Magic after he left Hogwarts and married Harry's mother.

In the next book, I think Harry goes back to Hogwarts but not Percy or the other Weasleys. Maybe in a future book Harry will grow up, and even get married. I'd like to see all the characters grow up and get famous, but not be in contact until they meet—they could have a reunion at Hogwarts.

I didn't see why Mrs. Norris had to die in the second book, even though no one liked her. Why didn't a person die, instead of a cat?

★　★　★

Laura Duell, 11 years old

Mysteries and puzzles appeal to me. I always try to figure out what's going to happen next in a story, and usually I can, but not in the Harry Potter books. There's a lot going on and you get caught up in the plot.

I don't think I'd like to go away to school. It would be pretty strange to sleep in a room with a lot of other kids all the time. Whenever my friends and I have sleepovers we never get any sleep. But if I could learn to be a wizard I would try it.

It would be better to fly on a hippogriff than a broomstick. It's easier to fall off a broomstick. And you could talk to the hippogriff, and feed him pumpkins and birdseed. I could keep him in the garage. I'd like to fly way up in the air and look down at the country.

Snape is really awful. It was funny when the magic map called him a slimeball and told him to wash his hair. I hope in the next book Sirius Black comes back and gets him kicked out of Hogwarts.

It's not common in the United States for children of grade-school and middle-school age to go away to boarding school, although it has always been part of the British educational system. But American children often go to sleepaway camp in the summer, so the idea of living away from home and parents is not new.

★   ★   ★

Sarah McKenna, 10 years old

Harry is like a real boy—except that he's a wizard! My favorite character is Hermione, because she's smart. Some of the boys like her because she *is* smart.

Quidditch is one of the best things in the books, and if I could play I'd want to be a Seeker.

I read the British version, too, as well as the American one, and didn't find it at all hard to read. I borrowed a copy from a friend who brought it back from England.

I don't exactly hate the Dursleys; I think they're funny. I also thought Dobby, the house elf, was funny.

I liked the way he got into trouble trying to protect Harry, and then Harry freed him.

I read an article that said that there are going to be seven books, one for every year Harry is at Hogwarts. I haven't read the third book yet, but I heard that in it a prisoner escapes from the wizard jail—I'll bet it's the Professor who teaches Defense Against the Dark Arts—and Harry catches him.

In the future books, I'd like to see Ron get a girl-friend.

I don't think I'm a Muggle—just because you're not a wizard doesn't mean you're a Muggle!

According to J. K. Rowling, the author of the Harry Potter books, there will be seven volumes, following Harry through each of his years at Hogwarts School of Witchcraft and Wizardry.

★   ★   ★

Mariel Klein,* 8 years old

The adventures were a little scary. That's what I liked about them.

Harry and Hermione were my favorites. And I like Dumbledore a lot. I really disliked Lockhart, especially because of what he did on Valentine's Day—sending out those disgusting cupids. He was too nice to Harry, and then he played tricks on him.

Hagrid is funny. I was glad when I found out that he went to school at Hogwarts.

Of the animals Scabbers is my favorite. I don't like things that pester people. Snape is mean. So are the Dursleys.

In the next book, I hope Harry goes home and the Dursleys are nice to him. I'd like to see another wizard or a new professor.

In Harry Potter and the Chamber of Secrets, *Gilderoy Lockhart is the new Defense Against the Dark Arts Professor. Children in both Britain and America often exchange Valentine greeting cards at school on Valentine's Day. In recent years, in fact, holidays like Valentine's Day and Halloween have become even more popular than Christmas or New Year's in this country.*

*See the Quidditch chapter for Mariel's comments about playing the game.

★   ★   ★

Rebecca Brown, 9 years old

The first book was the best one for me. I had trouble picturing what happened in the second book.

I liked Aunt Petunia and Dudley, because I could picture them. The part about going to Hogwarts, getting on the train at platform Nine and Three-Quarters.

I'm not sure if I'd like going away to school. If I

was Harry, of course, I would. And I guess I wouldn't miss home if I was having a good time at school.

My favorite part is where Harry puts on the invisibility cloak and sees himself and his family in the Mirror of Erised.

Most of the food sounds awful. He eats so much food, every day, and those yucky desserts! (I hate Jell-o.) I like the Chocolate Frogs, and I'd like to get a chocolate-mint Every Flavor Bean.

You're not really a Muggle if you're not a wizard.

In one of the next books I'd like to see Harry's parents come back and the Dursleys disappear.

To catch the train for Hogwarts, students must pass through a barrier between Platforms Nine and Ten to reach Platform Nine and Three-Quarters, which is invisible to anyone but wizards.

The Mirror of Erised shows to anyone who looks into it what it is he or she most desires.

★   ★   ★

Anna Holland, 13 years old

Fantasy and adventures are my favorite kind of reading. The plots of the Harry Potter books are complicated enough to be interesting.

Hermione can be nice sometimes, but some things she does are stupid—like telling the teacher about Harry's new broom in the third book. Sometimes she's just annoying. I didn't figure out how she solved the puzzle of the seven bottles at the end of the first book; I just trusted her judgment.

Of the animals, I liked Scabbers, because he was funny, although he wasn't good because he betrayed Harry's parents. I liked Ron's owl Errol, how he's so old and after he delivers a letter he just flops.

The Every Flavor Beans are a great idea, but I'd hate to get a snot-flavored one.

It's okay to be a Muggle if you believe in magic, but not if you don't, like Harry's uncle and aunt.

It's true that Snape was awful, but it would be boring if he wasn't there.

There has never been such a popular children's book series with such complicated plotlines as the Harry Potter books. When J. K. Rowling tried to publish the first volume, she was turned down by a number of publishers who thought that it was too hard for children to understand. Adults often underestimate children's abilities to follow a plot!

Katy Lisle, 11 years old

Harry seems like a friend. He kept talking Ron and Hermione out of being so mad at each other.

Dumbledore was amazing. He was silly and wise at the same time. And I think he's probably the most powerful wizard in the world.

Quidditch sounds great. I'd love to be able to fly. But I don't think you could play it here, on the ground; that would spoil it.

Lockhart was dumb and irritating. My grandma, she's a music teacher, said he reminded her of Liberace, this pianist who was on TV when she was young. He had a white fur coat and smiled a lot. But she said at least he could play the piano. Lockhart is a big phony as a wizard.

I play the piano, too, and I love music. I liked the way Dumbledore had everybody sing the school song to whatever tune they wanted, and it came out all right.

Albus Dumbledore, Headmaster of Hogwarts, is reputed to be the only wizard Voldemort is afraid of. Dueling wizards are not a new concept; in fact, much of the history of magic is about the counterspells and countersigns that wizards have devised to defend themselves from the attacks of their enemies. We have all read about the silver bullets and wooden stakes that are thought to be antidotes to certain supernatural dangers.

★   ★   ★

Adam Holland,* 8 years old

Lots of books are interesting at the beginning but then just fade off, but I liked these books because they kept on being exciting.

My favorite character is Dumbledore, and I like Ron Weasley. Hermione is OK, but not my favorite.

Quidditch is cool.

Of the animals, I like Harry's owl Hedwig, and the little owl Ron gets at the end of the third book.

The books aren't really scary, just scary enough.

I did figure out some of the puzzles, about how it was Black who gave Harry the Firebolt, and about the Invisibility Cloak.

The bad characters were Snape, Mrs. Norris or Malfoy. Snape is mean because he's on the Slytherins' team and doesn't like Harry or his parents.

I didn't like the Dursleys, and it was funny when Harry exploded Aunt Marge.

In the next books, I'd like to see more about Quidditch.

Harry's owl, Hedwig, which was an eleventh-birthday present given him by Hagrid, is a large, snowy owl with a curved beak and an affectionate disposition. Owls are creatures that fascinate children, perhaps because they are so seldom seen that they seem strange and scary. But in the Harry Potter books, owls lose their scary image because they are the children's friends and pets.

*See the Quidditch chapter for Adam's comments about playing the game.

Nurya Gilbert, 11 years old

The books are very clever. They fit together like a puzzle. I found them so fascinating I couldn't put them down.

The characters were all interesting and likable, although Hermione's kind of a goody-goody. I liked the teachers, and Dumbledore. I liked Hagrid. I picture him with longish hair sticking out from his head; he's not too tall, not too short.

Me, I'm not a wizard. I like being a Muggle—nobody expects anything much from Muggles.

Some parts of the books are scary, but they're also funny. When I was scared I made myself believe it was supposed to be funny so I wasn't too scared. The Whomping Willow was the scariest.

The magic car in the second book was like an unreliable friend.

I didn't like Lockhart; he was stupid. I couldn't understand the Dursleys. They seemed extreme. I felt bad for Harry that he had to live with them.

It would be scary if someone you knew had magical powers.

In future books I'd like to see more of He-Who-Can't-Be-Named. I really loved Dobby, the house elf in the second book, and I'd like to see more about him now that Harry has set him free. And I'd like to know how his master is getting along without Dobby!

I'd like to hear more in general about everything.

I wish the Dursleys could start to love Harry, or else he could get rid of them altogether.

Kyle Sargent, 9 years old

I like mysteries. I guess you couldn't really call the Harry Potter books mysteries, but they do have suspense.

Hagrid was one of my favorite characters, because he was gentle and kind. Hagrid is big and tall and hairy, with a beard that comes up around his nose. Snape and Quirrell scared me.

Harry's parents were killed by Voldemort, but maybe they might come back in a later book. I think his mom was probably a housewife and did the chores. I guess they lived in the wizard world, because they knew Hagrid.

Of the animals, I liked Hedwig. Hedwig was a really important character. The story wouldn't have been as good without Hedwig.

The food sounds like it tastes good. I'd like a chocolate Every Flavor Bean.

Quidditch sounds great, but it couldn't be played on the ground.

I did figure out some of the puzzles. I figured out some of the clues for the problem with the bottles at the end of the first book, but there were too many bottles and I couldn't get them all. I do play chess, and I knew that someone would have to be taken out of the game, as Ron was.

The Dursleys aren't nice. They might get a lesson at the end of the books. Snape is mean to Harry because he hated his father, but he didn't kill Harry so he might be friends with him in the end.

I would like to go to wizard school. I could get along, although I might cry some from being away from home, but it would be fun to ride a broomstick and learn how to turn things into dragons and stuff.

In the next books, I hope that Harry will be more connected with Sirius Black, and maybe move in with him like they talked about in the end of the third book. I hope Black won't be just a nice person to write to.

In future books, I'd like to see more of Snape and Black, because they're the bad guys and it's not really a story without bad guys. I think Quirrell should come back in again, too. And I think it should become a tradition that Dark Arts teachers get replaced every year.

I liked the books so much that I couldn't stop reading them. My mom read them to me, and I wouldn't let her stop because I got so worried and excited about what was going to happen next.

Shanti Sontag, 13 years old

I wish I could do magic. Not just like making people rise up into the air, but real magic like turning them into newts and frogs. And making people do something, or stop doing something.

I'd love to have a unicorn for a pet. I was sorry there wasn't more about unicorns in the book. They're really beautiful, and magical. The only unicorn in the books was killed, and Voldemort drank its blood to make him stronger.

I liked Hermione. She didn't let anybody push her around, not even Ron. And she had a lot of faith in her cat, Crookshanks, even when Ron said it was attacking his rat, Scabbers. I thought for a while that Crookshanks was the spy, but it turned out to be Scabbers.

The food sounds really awful. I'm a vegetarian, and all they ever eat is meat. The Every Flavor Beans sound interesting, though. What if somebody who hates vegetables got an eggplant one, or squash? I hope they didn't have beef-flavored ones. Eew!

The Dursleys were like cartoon characters, big and fat and nasty. They were funny.

I hope Sirius Black comes back in the next book, and there's a unicorn.

More and more American children are becoming vegetarians. It's part of our New Age culture. Britain is traditionally the land of beefeaters, and the food pictured in British books is mostly the sort of things vegetarians would not eat. But things are changing. There are an increasing number of organic farms, and restaurants that serve beautiful salad and vegetable dishes.

★　★　★

Daniel Astrachan,* 9 years old

Mysteries and magic are wonderful. I liked it when Harry and his friends got into trouble because they were using magic—like when Harry played tricks on his cousin Dudley, and blew up Aunt Marge.

I especially like Lord Voldemort and Sirius Black. They're mean, but Harry beats them even though they put up a real fight.

The giant spiders in the second book were exciting. And I like Hagrid because he's into monsters and dragons, and brought home the dragon egg to hatch out. I'd like to have a dragon as a pet.

Of the animals, the best were the dragons, and the basilisk, and the owls. I didn't quite understand how the owls knew where to go with the mail. And it's embarrassing when the owls bring somebody a red letter with a Howler in it!

Quidditch is a cool sport. I'd like to be Captain of a Quidditch team, because I'd like to plan the strategy.

I tried to figure out the puzzles. I thought I figured out the problem with the seven bottles but I was wrong. I play chess, and I thought the chess game in book one was neat—I didn't expect what happened.

I don't like Malfoy and his friends, Crabbe and Goyle. And the Dursleys are not nice.

In the next books, I think Black will send a letter from the Azkaban jail and escape again. He'll almost kill Harry and then have to save him.

Howlers are messages of complaint, usually from parents or guardians to children at Hogwarts, to scold them for doing something naughty or breaking the rules. Children who go away to boarding school are fortunate, actually, in comparison with those who live at home during the school year. At home, children must face up to scoldings right away, face to face with their parents, and sometimes in front of their siblings and friends, which can be downright embarrassing.

*See the Quidditch chapter for Daniel's comments about playing the game.

Julie Shapiro, 13 years old

I read the first book and really liked it, but I'm kind of an advanced reader and it seemed a little too young for me. But I thought it was well written and cute.

I expected it to be like other kids' books, but she (the author) had some unusual plots. The characters seemed to be real, although the Dursleys were a bit exaggerated. Snape was good, though; not exaggerated.

The Quidditch game sounds like fun. I like the idea of the Every Flavor Beans.

I'd recommend the books to fifth and sixth graders—they're fun, exciting, not too slow or shallow, with funny characters. Harry has more depth than most characters.

I liked it when the bad guys were in the woods, and killed the unicorn and Voldemort drank its blood, but they got stopped by the centaurs and Harry watched the whole thing.

Even older children, such as this advanced reader, enjoy the Harry Potter books because they are well-written and gripping stories. Author J. K. Rowling never talks down to children; however, many of her references can be understood on a deeper level by older children. She has promised that future books will follow Harry through to the age of 18, so older readers like Julie will find those books even more interesting.

★ ★ ★

Catherine Gannascoli, 9 years old

I read the first book and half of the second one. I like Harry because he gets into mischief with his friends Ron and Hermione and that makes him who he is. I like Hermione because she's smart—she always puts things right.

Nearly Headless Nick is a good character. So is Snape; although he can be mean, he saves Harry from stuff. He's mean because he doesn't like Harry.

My favorite character is Hermione, not just because she's a girl like me, but because she helps Harry and Ron get into stuff.

I like Harry because he's the main character, and because he could do stuff he didn't know he could do.

I really, really like magic. I guess I'm a Muggle because I can't do magic. Ron wasn't as good at magic as the others, and he doesn't really fit in with the smart kids because he's not as smart. He couldn't make as good disappearances as Harry and Hermione.

I'd like to go to wizard school, learn magic and put spells on people. I'd make up an ugly spell, and then—it's payback time! I'd turn people into witches with big warts on their faces, with two little hairs sticking out in different directions.

My favorite animal is Hedwig. I don't like Ron's rat, Scabbers, because I don't like rats.

Quidditch is a great game for wizards and witches. I'd like to play it, but it could be scary. I can't picture playing it on the ground; it would be too easy.

I'd like to have Every Flavor Beans in flavors like spinach and green beans—to taste but not really have to eat them. I'd also like them flavored like lemon drops and mints. I don't think the Chocolate Frogs are much different from the candy we have.

I didn't solve the problems in *The Sorcerer's Stone* because it moved so fast. My mom read it to me and I didn't figure it out while she was reading.

I don't like the Dursleys, Quirrell or You-Know-Who.

In the next books, I'd like to see more about Harry's parents.

★ ★ ★

Emma Steinberg, 12 years old

When you think of Harry and his friends, they aren't your typical book characters, even in fantasy books. The Harry Potter books have a special characteristic that makes them all different, yet so alike. That is why I like them.

A fun thing about being a wizard is, if you think about it, no two are alike and no one can do something the same way you do. Whereas in the Muggle world, people tend to do a lot of things the same way.

I would like to go to wizardry school because it would be really different from normal school and it would be like getting a taste of a totally different culture, more like the world we live in.

Quidditch on ground seems to me like a version of Dodgeball, in a way. The reason I think this is because there are a lot of different balls you have to throw or do something else with. Also, maybe not in the next book but after that it could be about Harry and his friends when they are older, like in their teens.

Going to wizard school was certainly an eye-opener for Harry Potter. He had never seen so many different children from so many different backgrounds, but what was even more amazing was the variety of magical people and creatures he met.

★ ★ ★

Charlie Johnson, 9 years old

Harry stands up to people like Malfoy. He's brave, even though he doesn't have a father or a mother. I also like him because he looks like me— I have black hair and wear glasses and I have a little scar on my forehead, that I got when I had the chicken pox. It's very small and doesn't look like lightning, though.

Hermione is neat because she's smart, and nobody makes her feel bad because she is smart.

I'd be kind of afraid about going away to school, but I'd love to learn magic. I could turn bad people into squirrels and pigeons so they couldn't do anything to other people.

Snape seemed like a really bad guy at the beginning, but then he saved Harry from Quirrell. He may be mean but I think he secretly likes Harry.

I hope Harry's parents come back in the next book.

Harry Potter is skinny, with knobby knees and black untidy hair that sticks up. He wears glasses over his bright-green eyes.

★ ★ ★

Sarah Goldstein,* 9 years old

The best things about the books are the magic, the sports and the culture (of the magic world).

Hermione is my favorite because she's smart, although kids sometimes think she's too smart. Ron is funny; that's his nature.

I want to learn magic, so I'd like to go to wizard school. I'd like to be able to put voodoo on bullies and enemies.

Dobby the elf is one of my favorite characters. I like Peeves; he was a poltergeist, but he was like an elf, too. It was funny when he tried to put gum in keyholes and the gum went up his nose.

I love the Every Flavor Beans, but I'd hate to get a booger-flavored one, or vomit or earwax!

It's probably true that everyone who isn't a wizard is a Muggle, just going about their everyday lives, but that's okay.

I solved the puzzle of the seven bottles in the first book. I play chess, and really liked the chess games, but I didn't expect what happened in the one at the end of the first book.

Snape isn't nice, but he was just doing his job, and he had to be strict.

I think Harry's parents made potions and sold wizard stuff for a living.

In the next book I would like to see Snape die—it would be like a miracle, because he's so mean to Harry.

See the Quidditch chapter for Sarah's comments about playing the game.

★ ★ ★

Dylan McKenna, 10 years old

I only read the first book, but I really liked it because it was humorous and interesting, too.

Harry is my favorite because he's a wizard and powerful, and because he managed to stay alive when his parents died.

I want to go to wizard school and learn magic. I'd like to learn to use a wand to cast spells. Then I would turn my brother into a toad. I'd like to be able to do the leg-lock, so someone couldn't move.

The Every Flavor Beans are pretty weird. A chocolate or toffee one would be good, but not earwax or booger.

I didn't figure out the puzzles. I let Hermione do that.

The kid in Harry's family, Dudley, and everyone in that family, were my least favorites. Snape was mean because he knew he had to make up for

Harry's father saving his life, but he didn't know how to do it.

I liked Hagrid. He was a giant, but he was still nice.

All kids have a lively fantasy life, which keeps them open to all kinds of possibilities—such as magic. It doesn't seem to them too unlikely that someone could cast a magic spell that would turn another person into a toad, or that would cause a pot of flowers to fall off a windowsill and knock an enemy on the head.

★   ★   ★

Jessica Widman, 10 years old

It would be great to have teachers like the ones at Hogwarts, and I like what the kids study. Herbology is like gardening. It was neat when they repotted the mandrakes. I laughed when the teacher said he knew the mandrakes were growing up because they kept trying to get into each other's pots. That's like my older sister and her friends, always wanting to be together.

I'd love to go to wizard school. Then I wouldn't have to go on the school bus where the other kids are such a nuisance, and I wouldn't have to listen to my sister talking on the phone all the time to her boyfriend.

You could play Quidditch with badminton birds. Paint them three different colors and don't use a net.

My family and I play badminton when we go to the lake, and I'm going to get them to try it next summer.

I've never seen a real owl up close. I'd like to see Hedwig and Errol and the little owl Ron gets at the end of the third book.

One of the great things about reading fiction is that it takes you out of your ordinary world, and at the same time shows you how other people deal with the same problems you have. This perspective helps children develop new ways of approaching life.

★ ★ ★

Robby Rindlaub, 12 years old

I liked the books very much—the plots, and how they always got exciting towards the end, as they reached a climax. Some parts of the books I've read 10 or 15 times.

Harry isn't perfect, but he redeems himself in other ways.

Hagrid is nice but he looks mean. I like Snape, too, because in the first book you think he's the bad guy but it's really Quirrell. I like Snape because he's the ongoing bad guy.

Hermione seems nice; she certainly is a bossy mortal but she's okay.

It would be fun to go to wizard school, but it

almost seems like wizards aren't as smart as Muggles—
it takes wizards longer for them to talk to each other,
but Muggles just call each other up. But it's cool how
wizards have to hide it (their magic world) from the
Muggles.

The teachers sound eccentric. The Divination
teacher is very strange, but that's not a major draw-
back.

Quidditch sounds like fun, but it wouldn't work
well here because the balls wouldn't fly.

I had no idea how Hermione figured out the puzzle of the seven bottles. I didn't really think about it—
once you read it and know the answer it kind of
ruins the mystery of it.

I think the last book should have a major con-
frontation with Voldemort. He should be utterly
destroyed instead of just being turned into a vapor.

★ ★ ★

Jessie Kotansky, 12 years old

I liked everything about the books. I read a lot, and
most books don't have the quality of the Harry
Potter books. It's cool how Harry has two worlds—
the magic and the normal people.

Harry is a great character because he's famous but
he's really calm about it. He's like a normal person.

Hagrid was funny, nice and good.

I'd love to go to wizard school, and play Quidditch.

I've thought about how to play it, but haven't worked it out yet. I'd play the position of Keeper.

The owls and hippogriffs were my favorite animals; I can kind of picture them.

I'd like to get an Every Flavor Bean that tasted like cream soda. I'd hate to get a licorice one.

It's okay to be a Muggle. They have to be the way they are to be in the story.

The characters I didn't like were Malfoy, Voldemort, Snape, Crabbe and Goyle. Snape is mean because he's hard on all the Gryffindors, and because he's jealous of Harry. The Dursleys really didn't seem real.

In the next books, I'd like to see Snape get fired, Malfoy kicked out of school, and Harry go to live with Sirius Black.

Children who read as much as Jessie develop their abilities to focus on a topic and to think things through. He already shows signs of becoming an excellent literary critic. And teachers agree that the more children read, the better their writing skills become.

Brian Young,* 10 years old

If I got to go to wizard school, I'd like to take Muggles Studies. I think that would be really interesting, you know, to see what wizards think of ordinary people.

I haven't got a particular favorite character. I liked Hagrid; he was funny.

I was fond of the owls, especially the little one that Sirius Black gave to Ron at the end. It was cute.

Quidditch would be a really cool sport. If I played, I'd be a Beater, one of the players who keep the Bludgers off the other players.

The Every Flavor Beans were gross. If I had a choice I'd like to get one that tastes like vanilla ice cream with chocolate fudge sauce.

I didn't like Quirrell, Voldemort or Snape. Snape was mean because Harry's dad and his friends played a trick on him. And then, Harry's dad saved Snape's life so Snape was annoyed because he owed him.

I think Harry's parents worked at some wizard thing. Maybe his father did the commentary at Quidditch matches, because he was a great Quidditch player himself. They probably lived in the Muggle world, not near Hogwarts because someone would've known about it. The only place they could've lived at Hogwarts would be the Forbidden Forest, and it was too dangerous there.

In the next book I'd like to see Voldemort come back, as a flea or something. I'd like to see how broken-down Voldemort could get, if he returns to Hogwarts, what he docs to Harry and how Harry escapes.

The Dursleys were not nice—fat, cross little people (actually, not so little!). It was really funny when Harry blew up Aunt Marge.

I hope Harry goes to live with Sirius Black. Maybe

Black lives in the Shrieking Shack—there was furniture there. And Black has a hippogriff, so he can go wherever he wants.

I hope they use the Time-Turner charm again. I liked the Patronus spell Harry used on the dementors.

See the Quidditch chapter for Brian's comments about playing the game.

★   ★   ★

Sasha Rivera, 10 years old

What's best are: the dark castles and dungeons and Hagrid's hut and the creepy-crawly things like toads and the things in jars on the shelves. And Hagrid's pets, the things with three heads and wings and giant spiders and stuff.

I'd be scared but I'd like to go to wizard school. I'd sneak around at night in an invisibility cloak like Harry. I'd have a pet but I don't know what kind, maybe a toad. They don't eat much.

You could play Quidditch like field hockey, but everyone would have to remember which balls were the Quaffles, the Bludgers and the Snitch. They could be different sizes and painted different colors. I'd be a Chaser and get the Quaffles into the hoops while somebody else worried about the Snitch.

Maybe Harry's parents ran a wizard health club

and made potions to keep people from having aches and pains and to help them build up big muscles.

Harry receives the Cloak of Invisibility as a Christmas present from an unknown friend in the first book, and uses it to prowl around Hogwarts undetected. Who wouldn't love to roam unseen through the world, and see what other people are doing and saying? Perhaps they're talking about us, or people we know!

★　★　★

Harrison Weis Monsky,* 9 years old

I like the books because they're about things that aren't possible in our world. I couldn't wait to find out what's happening next, and I wanted to read more and more.

My favorites are Professor McGonagall, Harry and Hagrid. But I had trouble remembering what Mc-Gonagall looks like, after she was described at the beginning.

I think maybe in the fourth book we'll find out more about Harry's parents. I think they lived in the wizard world, because the Dursleys don't mention them, but wizard people are always talking about the Potters, and they were good friends with Dumbledore. Harry's father James was all wizard, and his mother must've been all Muggle because her sister Aunt Petunia was a Muggle.

Of all the owls, I liked Hedwig best. Hedwig is a small, regular owl, brown and gray in the middle with a yellow beak and claws. When she spreads her wings she looks bigger. Hippogriffs are really big and come in lots of different colors.

It wouldn't be good to play Quidditch on the ground; it'd be just running around with bats, and you couldn't have really high goalposts. And it would be easier for a Bludger to hit you.

I play chess a little and I solved the chess problem.

Lockhart was such a bad wizard! He made Harry's bones disconnect when he tried to cure his broken arm. The Dursleys get mad easily and it would be terrible to live with them. I have a hard time imagining what Dudley looks like. I picture Aunt Marge, the one Harry blew up, as big and fat and with a mustache.

I don't want anyone to die in the next book. It would be cool if Harry is allowed to use magic in the real world next year (his fourth). And I'd like to see him give Dudley another tail.

See the Quidditch chapter for Harrison's comments about playing the game.

Perrin Kirby, 9 years old

I liked the Chocolate Frogs. All the Every Flavor Beans would taste good.

The Dursleys are mean, fat and ugly. They eat candy a lot and they're enormous.

In the next book I want to learn everything about Harry. And more adventures, and more new kinds of magic, like pressing a button on a wall to make something happen.

I'd like to go to wizard school to learn magic, but it would be sad to leave my friends at home.

What's neat about the magic is the things in jars, and the dark, dirty chambers, with toads everywhere, and the rats. And the spells—I'd like to turn someone into a frog. I'd like to turn myself into a dog; I really like dogs. And I like Harry's owl.

I'd like to see the next books be more scary.

Chocolate Frogs are a kind of wizard candy. Wizards always seem to keep a lot of strange creatures around, in different states of preservation. Since the Middle Ages, scientists and magicians have been famous for storing frogs, toads, bats, homunculi and horrible mutant creatures, pickled in jars, on their shelves. Of course, these were merely specimens for study, but to the layman they were repulsive and scary.

Danny Marcusa, 8 years old

This is my type of book. There's a lot of action—once one mystery is over, there's a new mystery.

I like Hagrid. He's always in the middle of everything. Hermione is brainy.

I think Harry's dad, after he left Hogwarts, played Quidditch, was a star player and lived in the wizard world.

I'd like to go to wizard school, and study everything—except Potions, because I don't like Snape! He's mean because he's an archenemy of Harry's dad. He saved Harry in book one because Harry's dad saved him and he wanted to even the score and get that over with.

It would be very fun to play Quidditch. I'd like to be a Beater, and use the Bludgers to block other players.

My brother sat down and figured out the puzzle about "I am Tom Riddle."

I thought Voldemort was cool. I didn't like the Dursleys. Malfoy was a troublemaker.

I heard that the next book is about the Quidditch World Cup, and I think Gryffindor will face professional Quidditch teams.

The puzzle about Tom Riddle was an anagram, which is a word or phrase that can be unscrambled to reveal a secret message. There are many other kinds of word puzzles, like palindromes (sentences that read the same backwards or forwards, such as the one attributed to Napoleon: "Able was I ere I saw Elba") and word scrambles like the ones in this book.

Mike Marcus,* 10 years old

I read the British versions of the books. I got them from a friend who had been in England. They weren't hard to understand.

I liked Oliver Wood best. He was the Gryffindors' Quidditch Captain. I'd like to play Beater, like Fred and George Weasley.

I like Dobby, the elf. He was funny. I also liked Fawkes, the phoenix who helped Harry out with the sword and the hat in the second book. I think he followed Harry down the pipes from the bathroom to get to him.

I hate Snape more than Voldemort, because he's mean to Harry. I had a teacher pick on me once, and it was bad, and Snape reminded me of that and made me really mad.

I solved a mystery in the first book; I figured out that Quirrell was the bad guy when Harry saw him down under the trap door.

I'd hate to have parents like the Dursleys. I was mad that Harry didn't get to move in with Sirius Black and leave the Dursleys.

In the next book I'd like to see Gryffindor win the Quidditch Cup. I want to see Harry really confront Voldemort. I hope Snape gets kicked out of Hogwarts. I'm mad that Lupin left.

*See the Quidditch chapter for Mike's comments about playing the game.

Sophie Lazar,* 8 years old

My parents are getting me a dog and I'm going to name it Harry Potter!

It's surprising how Harry and his friends find time to do everything—go to school and have adventures and solve mysteries.

Hermione helps with everything. She makes spells—she's a human spelling dictionary!—and helps the others with their homework. She's not too smart, because she still has to study.

I like Harry and Ron, of course, and I also like Hagrid, Dumbledore, the Weasley twins Fred and George, and Madam Pomfrey (the nurse in charge of the hospital wing).

I loved Dobby the house elf. It was so funny when he'd hit his head on the wall, and once he hit himself over the head with a water bottle!

Quidditch is interesting. I root for different teams in different games, though I always want Gryffindor to beat Slytherin. But I rooted for Hufflepuff in one game.

Snape and Harry's father hated each other and so Snape hates Harry. Snape also hates the Gryffindors. I didn't like Malfoy or his father, either.

In the future, I'd like to see Voldemort put a spell on Hagrid so he does bad things and they take Hagrid to jail in Azkaban, but Voldemort gets caught by Harry and Voldemort gets put in Azkaban. In the seventh and last book, Voldemort should totally die.

Maybe Hermione shouldn't be so smart; then she'd be more interesting. She'd be more like Harry and Ron. But the whole book depends on her to get the right answers, so maybe she should be more smart instead of less smart.

Hedwig, Harry's owl, has a fun time soaring around and still does her job at the same time.

The books are special because you don't know at first there's going to be a mystery, but they're not boring at the beginning. They just keep you reading. There's something exciting happening in each chapter.

Dobby, the house elf who appears in the second book, is a great favorite with children.

Long ago, in the Middle Ages, every household needed servants to do the chores we now have done by machines. There were no vacuum cleaners, washing machines, gas or electric ovens, breadmakers or microwaves. There were no supermarkets, either, so householders stored huge amounts of food to be used for long periods of time, and someone had to protect the potatoes, onions, root vegetables, apples, dried fruits, dried meat and spices from mildew and decay. Gardeners were needed to grow food for the family's table. Clothes were elaborate and worn in many layers because houses were cold, heated only by fireplaces. So servants were needed to keep clothes clean and help the householders get dressed every day.

Servants usually lived with one family all their lifetime. If the family was kind and generous, their servants led a good life with plenty of food to eat and clothes to wear. But some masters were stingy or mean, and their servants led miserable lives.

*See the Quidditch chapter for Sophie's comments about the game.

★ ★ ★

Matthew Lebowitz, 10 years old

Even though Harry is always getting into trouble at Hogwarts he doesn't get thrown out. And when he does do something that gets him into trouble, I can see his reasoning.

Harry and Hermione are all that Hogwarts students talk about, and that's cool. Even if his friends don't want him to do something they support him anyway.

Hermione is sometimes a nuisance, but I like her anyway. I wouldn't like to be like her; I'd rather be more like Harry and Ron.

I'd want to go to wizard school if I was a wizard, but if I wasn't I wouldn't know what they were talking about. I would study Defense Against the Dark Arts, and Professor McGonagall's class, Transfiguration, and the extracurricular course on dueling.

Hippogriffs and owls were my favorite animals. The owls were neat when they flew right into the great hall and flapped around. I'd like to fly on a hippogriff if it was one that liked me, but if it didn't it could bite me because they can be vicious.

It was okay that Ron didn't have a new owl. Harry and Hermione had other pets, but Ron had Scabbers, the rat.

Quidditch is awesome, and scary. I'd be afraid I would break half the bones in my body. I admire Harry because he was good at it. I liked all Harry's brooms. I hope he gets another one in the next book.

I had trouble understanding what the third book was about when I started it, but it was so interesting that I kept on reading it until I did understand it. All the books kept me on the edge of my seat.

If I could do magic I'd like to make things appear and disappear. I'd like to make my sister disappear. I'd live in the lap of luxury. But you can't just make things appear by wanting to; you have to learn curses and things to make the spells work.

They should go on another big adventure in the next book. I'd like to see a new Defense Against the Dark Arts teacher, and more magic, and I'd like to see Harry win the Quidditch Cup.

★   ★   ★

Jeffrey Morse, 11 years old

There is really nothing else like the Harry Potter books!

Harry's father is mentioned a bit more than his mother because he played an important role at Hogwarts.

There are so many different spells in the books. Hermione knows how to do them all because she's a great wizard who studies a lot. I think the potions are made up of interesting combinations of all kinds of stuff.

It would be great to be a wizard because you could control situations and things like teachers.

The books are not as scary as they are exciting. Each new adventure takes a surprising turn of events for Harry and his friends.

Owls are my favorites. They help the characters because they transport letters and information. The hippogriffs are cool, too, because they are a mix of horses and eagles.

The Quidditch matches are fun to read about. I play soccer, which is kind of like it. Our ball is like the Quaffle, but the ball goes into a goal instead of a hoop.

The food sounds really good, especially the treacle fudge. But the Every Flavor Beans could be made of vomit, and ghost food sounds horrible because it's really old.

I solved the puzzles from the clues written into the stories.

The Dursleys were awful because they didn't understand how helpful Harry could be and they hate him for no reason.

The next book should be about Peter Pettigrew and Voldemort coming back to try to kill Harry.

Justin Spees, 12 years old

In the Harry Potter books the main plot is written in a way that makes you want to keep reading. Harry's adventures aren't scary, as much as they are tense.

I like Peeves the Poltergeist because he is the comic relief!—and the owls because they are very useful to Harry and his friends. I love the sound of the food and would like to eat the desserts!

We play soccer and basketball, though Quidditch is more exciting and I would love to play it.

Not everybody has to be a Muggle. If you show special talents you can be a wizard.

I figured out the puzzles because they are related to things I've done at school, like word searches, and solving word problems and riddles.

The books are kind of typical Good-versus-Evil stories, but it would be more fun if the plot was different.

The next book should be about how Voldemort rises to power.

★ ★ ★

Brianna Rose MacDonald, 12 years old

Harry and his friends aren't afraid to try new things, and not afraid to face danger, and they always stand up for each other. I absolutely adore Hagrid. My other favorites are Fred and George (the

Weasley twins). And Moaning Myrtle is so sad, but so funny. My favorite creature was Ron's owl, Errol.

You hear about Harry's dad a lot because he went to Hogwarts and so knew a lot of the characters from the early days.

I've always wanted to do magic, and I like the imagination used in describing Harry's world. The most fun thing about being a wizard is getting to go to Hogwarts. But people like me are not Muggles, because we know there is magic in the world.

The dementors were the scariest thing about the books. Everything else was just suspenseful.

If I had a broomstick, Quidditch would be less confusing to play. I'd love to try it, though.

The feasts at Hogwarts were wonderful. But my friends and I hate the Every Flavor Beans—we're afraid we'd get something disgusting.

We don't like the Dursleys, because they are cruel. Snape is mean sometimes, but only because he still feels hurt from being an uncool kid. He's good enough to save Harry when he should.

We don't know what's going to be in the next books, but we can't wait to find out. We like the author's writing because she makes magic seem real, and she creates interesting characters.

Josh Goetz, 7 years old

Harry is curious, like me, and he's lucky to be a wizard at Hogwarts.

Ghosts are really cool once you get to know them. Being a wizard would be great because I could play Quidditch and cast spells.

Harry's mysteries are frightening because once I get to a part that has a mystery in it I can't stop reading!

The owls are my favorites because they can carry letters to friends, and the cats because they're cute, and the hippogriffs because you could fly on them.

I love the food—I mean treacle fudge, Every Flavor Beans and Chocolate Frogs.

Snape is so mean to Harry because he hates Harry and is the manager for the Slytherin team.

J. K. Rowling should make two new characters who are father and son. The father teaches Defense Against the Dark Arts and the son is in Slytherin and both of them possess all kinds of powers over things like the Chamber of Secrets and the dementors in Azkaban. She should make up another Sorcerer's Stone, too!

Shunsuke Hirose,* 9 years old

If I had a broomstick I would ride it as soon as I learned how to, following what Harry Potter did.

It's fun that you can get Every Flavor Beans and Chocolate Frogs on the Hogwarts Express and at Hogsmeade.

I do *not* like the Dursleys, Severus Snape and any of the Defense Against the Dark Arts teachers, except Professor Lupin, who taught Harry the Patronus.

*See the Quidditch chapter for Shunsuke's comments about playing the game.

Ben Nissan, 8 years old

Norbert, the Norwegian Ridgeback, is my favorite animal in the Harry Potter books because he is a cute little fire-breathing dragon. But soon he's not that little!

Norbert is Hagrid's pet dragon. Hagrid hatched him from an egg. Pet dragons are illegal for wizards.

I liked thinking about what would happen to Norbert. I was happy that Norbert was safe with Ron Weasley's brother, Charlie.

Dragons are magical creatures with great power. They are usually described as enormous reptile-like monsters, with ridged spines, long tails, huge teeth and claws, that breathe smoke and fire. The first reports about dragons were written in the Middle Ages, but that may be simply the time when Europeans learned to write things down. Dragons may date back much farther than that. Some people believe that dragons are memories of the dinosaurs, implanted in humans' minds before the Ice Age.

In Greek mythology, the god Apollo destroyed a dragon named Python. One of the most famous dragons, a particularly nasty one that menaced young women in medieval England, was slain by St. George. In Chinese mythology, however, dragons bring good luck and help control the rainfall on crops.

★   ★   ★

David Morse,* 9 years old

It is fun to read about wizards and the adventures that Harry has, especially in dark chambers, and when he runs into bad guys like Voldemort. Harry and his friends usually get into trouble, while in most other stories it's the bad guys who get into trouble.

I like to hear about Quidditch. I play soccer, but we stay on the ground, not fly around. It surprised me that Harry fell and broke his arm in the game.

The food sounds great EXCEPT for the vomit Every Flavor Beans. I would like to see a popcorn wand that keeps popping out popcorn so you can eat it!

I don't know why Malfoy and Snape and Lucius had to be so mean to Harry.

The next book should be about Harry in a dark

cave meeting with Sirius Black, and every time Harry goes on an adventure he meets up with a bad guy. I think he should live with Hagrid, the Weasleys, Dumbledore or some good guy.

Playing Quidditch on the ground could be difficult. Players should be warned to be very careful about using golf balls, which are very small and hard, and baseball bats in their own versions of the game. Of course, it would be even more dangerous to play it while flying through the air, where players have to keep a watch above and below as well as in front, back and sideways!

*See the Quidditch chapter for David's comments about playing the game.

★   ★   ★

Jonathan Spees, 9 years old

The best things are the maps and word spells. It would be great if I could use the magic spells to make people disappear.

Hagrid is my favorite character because I like his accent and he is always so cheerful.

The owls are good because they're good mail carriers.

I love Quidditch. It is close to soccer, which I play a lot. Except that we play soccer on the ground.

The food appeals to me, even the Every Flavor Beans. I like the Chocolate Frogs, too.

I didn't like Lucius Malfoy so much. And I don't know how his son Draco Malfoy manages never to get expelled, because he does so many bad things.

The next book should be about how Malfoy gains a lot of power and becomes the new bad guy.

Hagrid's accent is a pleasant country way of talking. He's probably from the north of Britain, where author J. K. Rowling comes from. It is indeed a mystery how Draco Malfoy manages not to get expelled. But if you examine the facts objectively, he doesn't do anything more against the rules than Harry does.

Maps are often sources of mystery and intrigue. Pirates of the 16th, 17th and 18th centuries often buried their stolen treasure on Caribbean islands, leaving maps behind to puzzle their pursuers. Maps made by early explorers of the New World are fascinating, too.

★   ★   ★

Leah Rosen, 10 years old

I've been thinking a lot about Hagrid. He's my favorite character. I loved it when he came into the Dursleys' house on the motorcycle.

We know who Harry's parents are, and Ron's and Hermione's and Neville's, and you can sort of guess what kind of parents the teachers had. But we don't know what Hagrid's parents were like. I guess they were giants, but where did they live? Is there a giant village somewhere where they came from? Does he have any brothers or sisters? What if he wanted to get married?

I love the pink umbrella Hagrid carries around. It seems to be something like a magic wand. I guess Hagrid couldn't have a real magic wand because he was expelled from Hogwarts. But I think the umbrella has magical powers anyway.

I hope Hagrid gets to be Professor of Care of Magical Creatures again in the next book. It wasn't his fault that Buckbeak attacked Malfoy. And I hope he gets Buckbeak back.

Magic wands are an important part of a wizard's kit. They seem to be made of wood, usually a willowy kind of wood that makes them easy to wave in the air. Fairy godmothers such as Cinderella's, or Sleeping Beauty's, always had wands, to bestow beauty and other wonderful gifts on their protégés.

Jeffrey Schneider, 9 years old

The books are exciting and had a lot of suspense. Not much is scary about the adventures. The magic is neat and I really like the broomsticks best.

My favorite animal is the hippogriff Buckbeak, because he is awesome and people can get on his back and fly around.

I really like the Every Flavor Beans and the Chocolate Frogs. But I would only eat the Chocolate

Frogs. I wouldn't want to get some of the awful flavors in the Every Flavor Beans.

I didn't like the boring parts, like when Harry was in school and learning. I wish they had skipped that and we just read about the adventures.

★　★　★

Mara Cattrall, 12 years old

It's true that we live in the Muggle world, but I think some people might really turn out to be wizards if they had a chance to go to wizard school. I mean, lots of people have special powers, like ESP. I've heard about psychics who find lost children for the police. I do stuff sometimes and don't know how I did it, like getting a book to open at just the right page or saying the same word as someone else at the same time. So if I could go to wizard school to learn how, I might be able to do spells and potions and fly a broomstick.

I wish that Harry could go live with the Weasleys. He has lots of money in the wizard bank and he could help them out, and they could be like his family.

I liked Hermione's cat, Crookshanks. My cat, Earl Gray, has a flat face like Crookshanks's, and he's very cute. But he's gray, not orange (like Hermione's cat, Crookshanks).

I hope Harry wins the Quidditch World Cup in the next book.

Peter Stanley, 8 years old

I wish I could go with Harry to dark chambers and tunnels and have adventures like he does. I'd be glad Harry was with me to fight against Voldemort and Snape and people like that. They would scare me.

I don't know how the dementors can kiss you if they don't have faces. They didn't scare me as much because they don't attack you. You just put a Patronus charm on them.

Also, I got confused about whether Sirius Black was a bad guy or not. He killed a lot of people and attacked Ron, but then they said he didn't do it. They said he got Harry's parents killed, but then they said it was the rat that did that. Maybe I'll get my dad to read me that part again.

The Patronus is a spirit made up of good, happy feelings that can counteract the evil, angry feelings projected by the dementors.

Casting magic charms or spells is similar to creating a mental state that will influence others to do what we wish them to do. We practice this every day, by using polite remarks, such as "excuse me," "please" and "thank you," to charm others into being cooperative with us. Thinking positive thoughts also helps us to keep from being thrown off course by the anger or resistance of other people. So it's easy to see that wizards have a good grasp of how human minds work!

Patricia Slonimsky, 11 years old

The way Harry and his Quidditch teammates fly through the air is the best magic in the books. This is my second year in gymnastics and it feels like flying sometimes. Some of my friends and I tried to make up a way to play Quidditch doing flips and cartwheels and stuff. It doesn't work very well because you're too busy turning over to grab a ball. But I think if you were very, very good you might be able to do it.

The hippogriffs are my favorite animals because they can fly. If I could be an animagus I'd turn myself into a bird, like a hawk or an eagle, and soar around spying on people. I'd know everything that was going on and I could tell my friends so they could do magic like the animagi (who could turn themselves into creatures like a wolf, a rat, a dog and a stag).

I love how whenever Harry and his friends get sick or hurt they get chocolate. I told my mom about that, but she said that orange juice is better for you. Rats!

I hope Harry doesn't get a girlfriend in the next book because I want to be his girlfriend someday.

Patrick Kellaher, 11 years old

It would be good to have friends like Harry, Ron, Hermione and Hagrid. If I could only fly on a broomstick! I'll bet it's not easy. I want to try to use a wand, do spells, make potions, and meet ghosts and elves. My favorite adventures are in the secret passages and sneaking around through tunnels.

Quidditch looks like fun. I'd like to be a Seeker, but if I couldn't get that position I'd like to be a Beater.

The Every Flavor Beans are not that appetizing. I'd like to try the Chocolate Frogs, the stoat sandwiches and the treacle fudge.

There are Muggles and wizards in the world. If you don't want to be a Muggle you have to learn to perform magic, and cast spells on people.

Indeed, it's not easy to fly on a broomstick. From the earliest days, witches have had trouble with their broomsticks. They put spells on each other's broomsticks, to make the rider fall off or the broom fly in the wrong direction. Or they hid a broomstick to keep a witch from doing what she wished to do. But a really professional witch would simply go out to the woods, cut off a likely twig, pronounce a magical incantation and create for herself a new broom.

Molly Christensen, 8 years old

Harry Potter and the Sorcerer's Stone was the first book I ever read from beginning to end that didn't have pictures in it. My mom couldn't believe it. I loved the book and I love Harry. I want to have a friend like him. I also want to go to the wizard school and learn lots of magic spells and stuff like that. The only bad thing about the book is that you wish you could do the stuff they do in the book, or you wish that you could actually be one of the people in the book, but you can't. I felt so bad for Harry at the beginning of the book because his parents were dead. I kept thinking how I would feel if my parents were dead. I think I felt worse than Harry did! Also, I really hate the Dursleys. They are like the mean stepmother in Cinderella. And if Dudley was my cousin, I would cast a magic spell on him and turn him into stone. That would teach him to be a nicer person, maybe. He made me the maddest of anyone in the book because he is just so mean. One more thing, I would love to have an invisibility cloak. I could spy on people.

★ ★ ★

Don Ward, 13 years old

Harry Potter is my idea of a good read. A good mix of scary and funny. The Hogwarts castle is like a good computer game, where you don't know where you're going next but getting there is fun.

I like the way you can never be sure if people are good or bad until you really get to know them. Or they're good but they're still kind of dangerous, like Hagrid and his animals. Or people are unfriendly and kind of crazy, like Snape, but you wish they weren't. I want to know why he hates Harry so much. And I want to know Harry's father, James. Maybe Harry will get to know him through being able to call up James's stag, like he does at the end of the third book.

I don't like why some people are afraid to let their children read the books. They think it'll make kids bad to read about magic. Everybody knows magic isn't real but that doesn't make Halloween bad. Just 'cause the books are exciting doesn't make them dangerous.

I think the books are good. They make me think about people and what makes them act the way they do. Most of the bad things that happened so far are because the people are scared of magic, like the Dursleys. The whole thing in the third book about Sirius Black turns out to be because nobody knows all the facts. That was confusing but exciting, finding out Professor Lupin was a werewolf and Scabbers was a person. And going back and changing time to save the hippogriff. I had to read that part twice to figure out how it worked.

I can't wait to see what happens next. I'm not really a sports fan so I can't figure out how the next book will keep me interested. I mean, I like hearing about Quidditch but I don't think a whole book about it can be as good.

I like Fred and George: They're like a good comedy team like one I saw in an improvised comedy show in New York. They put a new slant on everything they see. They make up for the way some people in the books are so serious, like Hermione and Ron.

★ ★ ★

Buddy Merrick, 11 years old

The third book was the best, although of course I'll probably like the fourth one even better, when it comes out. The way Sirius Black went from being a really, really bad guy to being a friend of Harry's was good. I have a godfather who is also my mother's cousin, and I like him a lot. He says there are some places you can't go without a kid, like ball games and the zoo, and so he takes me along. Of course, he never got into any kind of trouble like Sirius Black did. I got Jake, my godfather, to read the Harry Potter books and we talked about them. He says his favorite character is Professor Lupin, because he (Jake) always wanted to be a werewolf.

Jake and I like the food they eat at Hogwarts, the steak and roast beef and pies. He says that Chocolate Frog wizard cards are like baseball cards kids used to get when they bought bubble gum, and now they're worth a lot of money. Maybe Ron Weasley will get rich someday with the wizard cards he collects.

The flying—on broomsticks and on hippogriffs—is my favorite thing about the books. I want to learn to fly an airplane someday, and become a pilot like my dad. It would be even neater to be able to fly without an airplane!

You might be able to play Quidditch wearing the one-man flight packs they use in the Navy. They don't last very long so you'd have to fly down to the ground and get a replacement every once in a while. Also, you can't zoom around as much as Harry and his team do. But I'd like to try it.

2

Dear Harry...

LETTERS WE HAVE WRITTEN IN SCHOOL

Students in the sixth-grade class of Carmen Lopez are avid readers of the Harry Potter books. When Ms. Lopez assigned the class the project of writing letters to Harry, this is what some of them wrote.

Dear Harry,

I hope you did not have such a bad summer as the year before. Did you go to the Quidditch World Cup match with Ron Weasley? It's too bad that you didn't get to go to live with Mr. Black.

If you had stayed on the hippogriff when you rescued Mr. Black you could have gone away with him. In his letter to you, he said he was safe from the dementors, so you would have been, too.

You should take Muggle Studies next year at Hogwarts. You would learn about us here in America, I'll bet. Wizards could have a lot more fun here than in England because there's lots of woods for magical creatures to live in and no one would make you eat all that meat and boiled potatoes and stuff. We eat lots of fishes and vegetables and fruits.

If you ever come to America please come here to visit us.

Sincerely,
Andrea Brant

★　★　★

Dear Harry,

I wish I had an owl like you do. I would really rather have a magical cat or rat, though. They would be more fun to pet and hug than an owl. If I had a magical pet I would hide him in my room and he would cast a spell to keep my mom and my sisters out of the room. Then I would take him to school in my pocket like Ron Weasley and Scabbers, and he would make all my answers on tests come out right. He could do my homework, too.

I hope that you have a good year and win the Quidditch Cup again.

Sincerely,
Carl Kramer

Dear Harry,

It must be hard to go to wizard school. You have to learn so many different things, like casting spells, mixing potions, raising plants and duelling with wands. What is arithmancy? Is it doing arithmetic by magic? I would really like to learn how to do it.

Your friend Hermione is really smart. I wish I knew her. I would like to be her friend. You should tell Ron to be nicer to her.

I would like to be able to fly on a broomstick like you. I would fly all around the country and see what was going on. If something looked interesting I would come down and look into it. Then I would get up again and come home, and nobody would know where I had been.

Please be careful and don't break your arm again.

Sincerely,
Jane Arlino

★ ★ ★

Dear Harry,

I think Quidditch is the coolest game I ever heard of. You are lucky you get to play it. If I could play I would be a Seeker like you. I would fly around and watch the game and wait, and then I'd see the Golden Snitch and grab it! And make 150 points for my team.

I heard that the next book is all about Quidditch and that there are other wizard schools in it. So I guess you will be playing their teams. This will be scary because you don't know the other teams and the other players. And you won't have Oliver Wood as Captain because last year was his last year at Hogwarts. You will have to be very clever. It would help if you could get someone to go to the other schools' Quidditch matches and come back and tell you about how they play. Then you can plan your strategy.

Good luck!

Sincerely,
Buddy Sinclair

★ ★ ★

Dear Harry,

I wish I could make things appear and disappear like you do. And I wish I could do a Patronus on my music teacher because he scares me like a dementor.

Here's something else I wish. I wish I had a pet hippogriff. It would be able to make itself invisible so it could go everywhere with me. Then we would sneak out in the middle of the night and go to faraway places. We might even go to England and visit Hogwarts. I would call it Pog, which is in the middle of the word hippogriff, and feed it sawdust from my dad's shop and food left over from dinner. It would love me and tell me good things like how I'm smarter or more grown-up than other kids. We would have a secret language no one else could understand.

Please tell Sirius Black to send me his hippogriff when he's through with it.

Sincerely,
Anne Marie Gunther

★ ★ ★

Dear Harry,

You have such a cool life and I wish I could, too. You may not be cute but you're really good at Quidditch and everybody admires you. Hermione thinks she's so smart but she is stupid to criticize you.

I would like to be able to do magic and make myself older so I could go to parties and stuff. If I could do magic I would make my hair all dazzly gold and put sparkly green stuff around my eyes. Then I'd have a magic dress that changes color every five minutes. People would think I'm a star like Brittany or someone like that.

I hope that you get to put a spell on the Dursleys soon and make them look really stupid. Good luck in your next book.

Sincerely,
Angelica Adorney

Dear Harry,

I and my friends admire you very much. You don't have any family alive that likes you, but you have made many friends and even the teachers seem to think you are special.

You live in a world where the most wonderful things happen. You fly on broomsticks and put spells on people and sneak out dragons and eat magic candy.

You play a game called Quidditch that has different balls and different players all flying through the air at the same time, and you always win the games.

I wish I could be like you and become a wizard and have a great time.

Sincerely,
Your Friend, Jack Hillburn

When Mrs. L. Maher asked her fifth-grade class if they had read the Harry Potter books, three hands shot up and three faces lit up with grins. When she asked the class to write letters to their favorite book character, the three children wrote the following letters to Harry Potter.

Dear Harry,

It must be exciting to be a wizard! Even before I read your books I always wanted to know so much about you.

Do you like your job as Seeker in Quidditch? What other job might you have liked? Your Nimbus Two Thousand seems really cool. I like your description of how it flies so high.

Your friends Ron and Hermione are really nice.

It was really brave of you to kill the mountain troll and fight Professor Quirrell.

I wish I could go to wizard school, too.

I'm looking forward to reading about your new adventures.

Sincerely,
Michelle Boutis

★ ★ ★

Dear Harry Potter,

I read your first adventure story and I really enjoyed it. I think it's interesting to read about normal people who suddenly can do fantastic things.

Is it hard being a wizard? If you went on a fourth adventure, where would it be? Who might you meet? Would there be new and more dangerous enemies? Would you have better magic to fight them?

I haven't started the second or third story yet, but I'm sure they are both just as good or better than the first.

Thanks for having the adventure. Without you, there would be no book.

Sincerely,
Jade Williams

Dear Harry Potter,

I have heard you have safely escaped from the Dark Lord, Voldemort. How does it feel to be wanted by a dangerous and powerful villain?

What do you expect in your later adventures?

Do you enjoy playing Quidditch? Who is your favorite teammate?

I've heard that you almost won the Quidditch Cup. Are you mad that you didn't win? I bet you're going to try harder next year.

Well, play safe and try not to get in trouble!

Sincerely,
Brian Jeong

P.S. How do you like your Nimbus Two Thousand?

Some students in the fourth-grade class taught by Andrew Thomas put in a special request to write letters to characters other than Harry Potter. Here's what they wrote:

Dear Hermione,

It's hard being smart. You are lucky that Harry and Ron want to be your friends.

I think you must be very pretty. You have curly brown hair and dark eyes. I am smart but I'm not pretty.

I like reading about your adventures. Why did you take so many classes in the last book? It was neat but you didn't need to do it.

You should not be so hard on Ron. He can't help it.

Best wishes to you in the next Harry Potter story.

Sincerely,
Cora Santucio

★ ★ ★

Dear Hagrid,

What is it like to be a giant? I would like to be taller than everyone else and look down at them. You could step on little people like they were bugs.

Why do you have that pink umbrella? I can't understand that.

I hope that you get to teach at Hogwarts again next year.

Sincerely,
Armand Saintelle

★ ★ ★

Dear Hermione,

I think you need to get a life. You keep your nose in a book and then you stick it into other people's business. I don't think it would be much fun to be your friend.

It is fun to read about what you do. I guess that in the next book you will do something different, like get a haircut and be Harry's girlfriend or learn to play Quidditch and be a star.

I can't wait to read the next Harry Potter book and see what you do.

Sincerely,
Tiffany Lifschitz

3

What Wizards Eat

RECIPES AND COMMENTS ABOUT
THE FOOD IN THE BOOKS

Food is an important matter in the lives of Harry Potter and his friends, as it is in the lives of all children. Some wizard food is strange, even weird, but a lot of it is perfectly delicious. After all, who would know better than a wizard—who can use his or her own scientific knowledge and supernatural lore—how to make things taste good?

One magic spell that anyone can use to make food wonderful is to make it look good when it is served. Diners will be charmed with the bright colors of fruits and vegetables, decorations like parsley or sprouts and lemon or tomato slices, or mounds of whipped cream and sprigs of mint on desserts. Arranging things in an interesting way on a plate is as good as putting a spell on it. One young cook laid out fruit salads on plates in the shape of a map of the United States. This same cook dyed applesauce blue, which was not such a good idea, because it was not appreciated by older members of the family. It's important to keep in mind the preferences of the people who are being served!

Wizard dishes can be traced back to the Middle Ages, when people in Europe lived mostly on meat and game. In those days, a feast might include dozens of different dishes, from fish baked with fruit to baked peacocks gilded with a coat of egg yolks to whole sides of roasted mutton and beef. There were delicious fresh fruits like figs, apples and pears. They drank hippocras, a refreshing beverage made of herbed wine, and they were served plenty of home-made bread to soak up the juices of their different courses. Witches and wizards knew the secret signifi-cance of foods, and would serve particular dishes in particular combinations to achieve a particular pur-pose. So when they cooked dinner, it was very much like mixing up a magic potion.

It's hard to imagine what some of the wizard food in the Harry Potter books tasted like, or how it was made, but a few Harry Potter readers have given it a try. Here are their ideas.

Treacle Fudge

My teacher said that treacle is the English word for molasses, and my mom has a recipe for molasses fudge that Grandma in Scotland gave her. We tried it and it's really good. So this is the recipe for treacle fudge.

>   1/2 cup light cream or evaporated milk
>   3/4 cup firmly packed dark brown sugar
>   1/4 teaspoon salt
>   4 ounces unsweetened chocolate
>   2 tablespoons (1/4 stick) unsalted butter
>   1/3 cup molasses (not blackstrap)

In a big bowl, mix together the cream, sugar and salt.

In a heavy saucepan, melt the chocolate with the butter. Remove from the heat and stir in the molasses.

Add the chocolate mixture to the cream mixture. Pour into a buttered 8 x 8" square pan. Let cool. Cut into squares and serve.

Mom says you can add 1/4 cup raisins, 1/4 cup chopped walnuts or a pinch of nutmeg if you want.

from Susanna McLaughlin, 13 years old

Stoat Sandwiches

My dad is a hunter and he likes to cook. He looked it up and he says that stoat is a kind of weasel and must be very tough. He thinks it might have a strong nasty flavor, too. So maybe it wasn't Hagrid's fault that they didn't taste very good. But here's what my dad says Hagrid would do to make his stoat sandwiches:

Have a game expert prepare the stoat and cut it up. Put the meat in a big pot with 2 cups each of red wine and vinegar, lots of sliced onions, some salt and pepper and a handful of pickling spices. Add enough water until the meat is covered. Cover and put in the refrigerator for a few days.

When you're ready to cook, take the pieces of stoat out, dry them off, dip them in flour and brown them in a little oil in a big pot. Strain the solids out of the soaking juice and add the juice to the stoat. Put on a lid, bring it to a boil and simmer until it's tender, for one or maybe even two hours.

Take the stoat out of the juice and, when it's cooled, remove the bones and slice the meat up for sandwiches. Use mayonnaise, mustard, lettuce, tomato and onion slices or whatever else you'd have on a chicken or hamburger sandwich. Sliced apples would be good, too. Whole-grain or dark bread would be the best bread to use.

from Billy Judd, 11 years old,
and his father, Alan

Stoat Sandwiches, and ...

Last summer my friend Chris and I made up a restaurant called Slimy Louie's, which serves stuff like Road Kill Stew, Arachnid Salad, French-fried Slugs, Possum Burgers, Cannibal Crepes Suzette and other stuff. All our friends came to our restaurant and we served them at the picnic table in our backyard. Then we read Harry Potter and added Stoat Sandwiches to our menu, and Rat-tat-tooy, and Toad in Aspic. Chris wanted to have Stuffed Owl but I didn't think that would be nice. You wouldn't want to eat Hedwig, or Errol.

from Ian Martin, 9 years old

Pumpkin Juice

I figured out how to make pumpkin juice like they drink at Hogwarts. My older sister Pamela helped me.

You start with a real pumpkin. First, you cut the pumpkin across in the middle and scrape out the seeds with a big spoon. Then you put both halves on a greased cookie sheet, cut-side down, and bake it in the oven at about 350°F. It may take up to an hour if it's a big pumpkin. Check it after a half-hour by sticking it with a fork. If it's soft enough for you to eat, it's done. It doesn't hurt to get it really soft, because then it's easier to get the pumpkin meat out of the shell.

Let the pumpkin cool down after you take it out of the oven. Scrape the pumpkin out of the shell with a big spoon.

Cut it into chunks and put them through the juicer. The juice we got had a pretty strong squashy flavor, so we added honey and apple juice and it turned out really tasty. Pamela says you could add milk instead of apple juice, but then you couldn't really call it pumpkin juice, could you?

from Shayla O'Reilly, 10 years old

Butterbeer

I like the name "Butterbeer" and wanted to taste it. I heard that some kids staged a protest against banning the Harry Potter books at their school and they made Butterbeer and drank it.

Here's how I tried to make it. First, I took some root beer and put some butter in it and heated it in the microwave until the butter melted. Then I stirred it and tried it. It tasted good, but it was warm and it wasn't fizzy anymore. Then I tried heating the butter first until it melted, heating the root beer just a little bit and stirring them together. That worked pretty well.

My friend Sancho thought we could melt down a

lot of butterscotch Life Savers, but they just melted into puddles and then got hard again when we took them out of the microwave.

We tried stirring the melted butter into ginger ale and it really tasted good, but I don't think you could call it Butterbeer. We tried putting cream in it, too, the kind they put in coffee, and that was even better. It was also good in the root beer. But again I don't think you could call it Butterbeer.

from Manny Mauricio, 9 years old

Christmas Plum Cake

For several centuries, families in Britain have enjoyed plum cake at Christmas dinner. British plum cake is very much like what Americans call fruitcake, for in England the word "plum" means prune or raisin. Plum cake, or plum pudding, which is nearly the same thing but steamed rather than baked, is often soaked in brandy or rum for months before it is served. And sometimes it is doused with brandy or rum again, at the end of Christmas dinner, and lit with a match so that it bursts into a lovely blue flame, which burns off the taste of the alcohol but leaves behind an especially rich and mellow flavor. It is traditional to stir silver charms into the plum cake before it is baked, so that at Christmas dinner each slice bears a fortune-telling charm, such as an animal or a toy or a symbol such as a heart, to bring special good luck to the person who receives it.

The cake our American friends have made here uses fresh plums, and it is very different from the British plum cake. But it is perfectly delicious. It could be made with any kind of fresh fruit, such as apples sliced thin.

My sisters and I wanted to try to make the plum cake for our family this Christmas, so we tried out some recipes and we came up with a really yummy cake. Here's our recipe:

> 1 plain white cake or pound cake that you
> buy in a store
> 1 tablespoon butter to grease the pie pan
> 1/2 cup sugar
> 1 teaspoon cinnamon
> 2 pounds Italian prune plums
> (you could use other kinds of plums)
> 1/2 cup melted butter

Preheat the oven to 350°F.

Butter a 9-inch pie pan.

Cut up the cake into thick slices and lay them out in the pie plate in one layer so you can't see the pan anywhere. If you have pieces left over, you can put them around the edges; they will help keep the plum juice from spilling out in the oven.

Mix the sugar and the cinnamon and spread most of it evenly over the cake in the pan.

Wash the plums, dry them and cut them in half.

Take out the pits. Cut the plum halves into nice neat slices.

Arrange the slices in circles in the pie pan to make one layer. The neater you do this, the prettier the cake will look when it's finished.

Pour the melted butter slowly over the plums so that all the plums get some. Sprinkle the rest of the cinnamon-sugar over the top.

Bake for 30 to 45 minutes. If the plum juice starts to boil up and over the sides of the pie pan, slide a cookie sheet onto the oven rack that's beneath it. It's done when the top is bubbly and a little crunchy.

from Mia Luna, 9 years old, and her sisters,
Alaia (12) and Liza (16) Luna

4

How We Play Quidditch

This aerial sport sounds as if it would be thrilling to play. It seems a little complicated at first, but as we read about it and began to picture the different balls and players in our minds, we came to understand it very well.

Some of us have tried to figure a way to play it here in our world. Here are our ideas.

Andrew Underberg, 12 years old

The game of Quidditch is a fantastic sport for both mind and body—it mystifies our minds and gets our adrenaline pumping. However, we do not live in a world where Nimbus Two Thousands or Golden Snitches exist. So, to play a game that seems utterly impossible without the use of fantasy equipment, some variations in the rules are needed.

A game that is true to the basic principles of Quidditch but is playable in the non-magic world has been created. It is called Roke (roe-key). Following is a list of the equipment required to play Roke. Their uses will be explained in the game rules.

Equipment:

> 1 Whingo (a whiffle ball)
> 1 Pinky (a small, soft rubber ball)
> 2 Roks (short stubby plastic bats)
> 2 Whimpers (wooden paddles, like those used in racketball)
> 2 Stoopers (bouncy paddles about the same size as those used in racketball)
> Some cones to mark out the goals
> A small field or yard or other space to play on

The rules below describe the way to play four-player Roke. It is possible to play Roke with more than four players. Extra players can be added to different roles, but it would be fairest to add the same number of players to both teams.

Rules of the Game:

1. The winning team is the first one to get ten points.

2. There are two players on a team and two teams.

3. There are two roles on each team:
   The Hurdler (like the Chaser in Quidditch), who uses the Rok to hit the Whingo.
   The Whacker (like a combination of the Bludger and Seeker in Quidditch), who uses the Whimper to hit the Pinky.

4. The Hurdler's job is to score points by using the Rok to hit the Whingo into the other team's goal for three points per goal, while using his Stooper to block the other team's Whacker from hitting him with the Pinky.

5. The Whacker's job is to score points by hitting the other team's Hurdler with the Pinky, using his or her Whimper. Each hit is worth one point. Also, the Whacker tries to protect his or her own Hurdler from getting hit with the other team's Pinky.
   However, there is only one Pinky in the field at a time, so the Whacker must try to get to it quickly.

6. It should be noted that the Whacker may not at any time have contact with the Whingo. If he or she does have contact with the Whingo in any way, he or she must hand over his or her team's Pinky to the other team's Whacker.

As in the Quidditch game played in the Harry Potter books, this Roke is fast and furious. The Hurdler must be very clever and agile to use both the Rok and the Stooper at the same time, and the Whacker must have quick reflexes to aim the Pinky and dodge the Whingo simultaneously. To add more players, you might try adding another Hurdler to each team and dividing the Hurdling job into two roles: chasing the Whingo into the goal, and defending against the Pinky. You could add another Whacker to each team, but you couldn't divide the role into two because both Whackers must avoid contact with the Whingo.

★ ★ ★

Ariel Doctoroff, age 9

I tried playing Quidditch with my sister and some friends when we were in Chicago. We used different kinds of balls. I was a Keeper and my friend was a Seeker. It would be fun to play Quidditch in airplanes, but they'd have to be open at the top so you could reach the balls. And you'd have to have really tall goalposts!

Mariel Klein, 8 years old

I tried playing Quidditch, by myself. I used a stick to bat a ball, and then I hid a little ball and pretended to find it.

Adam Holland, 8 years old

It would be hard for us to play, because you'd need flying balls—a Quaffle, three Bludgers and the Snitch—but it could be great as a computer game.

★   ★   ★

Daniel Astrachan, 9 years old

To play Quidditch here in the Muggle world, I think you'd need machines with strings that would move the balls. They could be powered by fuel for rocket ships.

★   ★   ★

Sarah Goldstein, 9 years old

I think you could play Quidditch on the ground. You could use basketball hoops and spray-paint one of the balls to be the Quaffle.

Brian Young, 10 years old

It would be very hard to play Quidditch where I live. Let's see, you'd need balls that fly around in the air and you'd need a big grassy meadow to play it in; there aren't many of those in my neighborhood. You could play it in airplanes, if you installed a grabber claw in each plane.

★ ★ ★

Harrison Weis Monsky, 9 years old

Quidditch is interesting, because it's played on broomsticks, and there are so many different balls and players. I like it that each ball has a different object, and each player has a different job. I think the stands must be very high, and get higher as the game rises up, but there's probably a boundary on how high it can go. It would be hard to see on a cloudy day; all you could see was players swooshing by.

★ ★ ★

Mike Marcus, 10 years old

Some friends and I talked about trying to play Quidditch. We'd use a golf ball as the Snitch, and soccer balls as Quaffles, and baseball bats.

Sophie Lazar, 8 years old

I think you could play it like a board game, with little brooms and people moving on squares. I couldn't figure out how to play it on the ground because you can't tell which ball is which.

Carolyn Singer Minott, 10 years old

I'd change the Quidditch rules: Bludgers can't hit Seekers or they get called on a foul. There should be a penalty box, and players should be taken off the field if they hit someone who can't be replaced. I think the school should provide the brooms so all the players have the same kind.

Emily Lebowitz, 14 years old

At camp, my friends and I thought about how to make a computer-animated version of Quidditch, but first we have to learn how to use the (animation) software. It wouldn't work on the ground, because the players would be running into each other all the time.

Carter Brown Grotta, 6 years old

We have Quidditch games. We stick stakes into the ground, and run around with sticks as broomsticks. We have other people playing, too.

We made a Golden Snitch by painting a tennis ball gold. We attached popsicle sticks to it like wings, and when it flies through the air they flap back and forth. It looks just like a real Golden Snitch.

★ ★ ★

Shunsuke Hirose, 9 years old

Here are my ground rules for playing Quidditch: No one can do damage to other teammates, opponents, the audience or the referee. Racing is not okay, although speeding toward the Snitch is all right. Blocking a penalty shot is illegal. Trying to curse a ball is illegal, if the wizard who does it gets caught. After what Professor Quirrell did to Harry Potter at the Gryffindor-versus-Slytherin game, Defense Against the Dark Arts teachers are not allowed at Quidditch matches.

David Morse, 9 years old

I would have a rule that wands would not be allowed in the place where a Quidditch game is going on.

★   ★   ★

Max Appleman, 11 years old

I had a few questions about the game of Quidditch. The Golden Snitch appears by magic in every game. But what if it didn't? Would they cancel the game? Also, could a Keeper or Catcher get the Snitch and pass it to the Seeker?

Maybe in the future books we will learn more about Quidditch. I heard that the next book will be called "The Quidditch World Cup." I can't wait to read it!

5

What Grown–Ups Say About the Harry Potter Books

Why and What Parents, Grandparents, Teachers and Booksellers Love About the Books

More and more grown-ups are reading the Harry Potter books, not just because their children are reading them, but because the books are so much fun! Here are some of the things grown-ups are saying.

Jane Lebowitz, parent and literary agent

From my perspective as a parent, I have a great appreciation for these books. My son is not an avid reader—he usually has to be pushed to pick up a book. I find it discouraging that he doesn't love reading as much as the rest of the family. So anything that super-sedes Nintendo and Pokemon is worthwhile to me!

Recently we took a trip to a bookstore to buy books for school. After we got Matthew his school books, he searched the shelves for a copy of the Harry Potter book he had been reading at home, found his place in it and sat down on a chair to read until the rest of the family was ready to leave. After he'd read the first volume, he couldn't wait to get his hands on the next one.

I couldn't believe the conversations between him and his friends about the books. One evening when one of his friends came to dinner with us, the kids spent the whole mealtime discussing the book. This kind of interaction takes the literary experience to the next level, beyond just reading it.

By the way, I find I use the word "Muggle" all the time! I think it's going to become part of our vocabulary.

Sometimes the kids pretend that they're wizards and that they're really in the books. On a certain level, the books have an appeal for kids that they don't have for adults. Kids understand certain things we can't. For example, I find some of Harry's experiences at Hogwarts frightening; I wouldn't want my child to go through such things. But the kids take it in stride.

I'm a literary agent and handle a number of children's books. I'm amazed that the author, J. K. Rowling, was able to invent all these things; I'm really impressed by her creativity.

The recent negative press about the books is hard for me to understand. In today's world, where people are sophisticated, educated and exposed to new ideas, such an attitude seems very old-fashioned. It's like something from the days of the Salem witchcraft trials.

★   ★   ★

Jennifer Ross, bookseller

These books are getting kids to read. Even kids who never liked to read before are now reading them. Any book that does that is an important book!

Adults like them, too. I've seen many parents and their children reading them together, or reading them separately and then talking about them together.

I'm a bookseller, and I ask every child who comes into the store if he or she has read the Harry Potter books. And I ask adults, too! Many people already have, of course. Often adults buy the books as presents for their children and grandchildren, and read them themselves before they give them away.

These books have brought more attention to the rather neglected field of children's fiction. For many years, it's been the beautifully illustrated books for small children that have gotten the most public attention, but that is quickly changing.

The books are so popular we can't keep them in stock. We recently got a shipment of the first-edition paperbacks of the first book, and they were sold out in a week.

I really like the books myself. I have to confess that I bought a copy of the third book from a little boy who was visiting here from England, and so I got to read it a week before it came out in the United States. (The boy had already read it, and said he could get another copy when he went home, so I didn't feel I was depriving him.)

★   ★   ★

Holly Singer Minott, parent

J. K. Rowling has a great deal of humor and imagination. She presents unusual things, like the Marauder's Map, as if they could really happen.

She is a careful writer, who obviously cares about her characters. They are well drawn, and there are so many of them! We counted 60 different characters in the first book alone.

Rowling places a lot of clues throughout the books, which helps the reader understand things better when they happen.

The books are important because they teach life lessons. The children in them try to be fair, which encourages the readers to do so, too. The books show children solving problems. They are not comfortable going to adults with their problems. That's empowering for children.

The children in these books use their own creativity and imagination to deal with things that trouble them, which is just what you want to teach kids. Grown-ups like teachers and parents need to make themselves obsolete in their children's lives, ultimately.

★ ★ ★

Laura Simon, grandmother

These books get children to use their imaginations to think differently. The kids' imaginations go wild when they read Harry Potter. The older you get, the less imagination you have; reading them put me in touch with being a kid again.

Kids don't have many mysteries in their lives. The books aren't really about witchcraft, but about mystery and magic, and that's new to the children. The books are somewhat scary, but kids like being scared.

As far as the critics who disapprove of magic and witchcraft are concerned, there were people who objected to The Wizard of Oz. And look what happened to that book!

Lots of frightening things in life are going to happen to children. If they can cope with what's in the Harry Potter books, which they know is made-up, they're a bit more prepared for life. If they can't separate the real from the imaginary, then of course parents shouldn't let them read it. But there are few children who fall into that category.

I have 13 grandchildren and I've bought copies of the books for all of them who are old enough to read them.

There are some interesting, lifelike subtleties that the author brings out. For example, Harry's aunt and uncle are probably not really awful people, but they're scared Harry will turn out to be like his parents, so they treat him badly.

★   ★   ★

Carmen Lopez, sixth-grade teacher

Reading is back in style, thanks to the Harry Potter books! Middle-grade students throughout our school are now reading on their own, and a number of children have discovered a new world in books, and are spending more and more time in the library.

The Harry Potter stories have an atmosphere of friendliness and fair play that is a good antidote to the violence they see on television and in the movies. The books help teach kids how to interact in a healthy way. The author takes on some serious topics, like ethnic cleansing, but deals with them allegorically, and within the context of the story.

Rowling is a fine writer and that provides a learning experience for the children. Also, they are exposed to a little bit of British culture. I've heard a number of children say they now want to visit England.

★   ★   ★

Carra Rockwood, fifth-grade teacher

I didn't know the books at all until my sister introduced me to them. As soon as I started reading them I adored them. I just devoured them—couldn't put them down.

Each book has a certain charm (no pun intended) of its own. As a teacher, I am gratified to see and hear that both children and adults are reading them. Adults don't always read children's books, but they are reading Harry Potter!

Every day after lunch, I have a sustained silent reading period for my class, lasting 15 to 30 minutes. I've noticed that more and more of my students are reading the Harry Potter books. The children's fascination with these books has sparked an interest in reading other books, as well. I see more kids coming to the library.

These are high-interest books because many children read and like them, and then share their enthusiasm with other children. It's a roller-coaster effect, kids picking them up from other kids.

The Harry Potter stories are unique because they show Harry growing up. Children get to know him as an eleven-year-old and then follow him as he gets older. Most children's books don't do this; their characters usually stay the same age, even in sequels.

The books give children some insight into a different kind of kid. They show a child from a difficult background finding himself in a new setting. And they encourage the children reading them to have a more positive attitude about themselves, and about their environment.

Any book that gets kids to read is a wonderful book. Also, I've noticed that as kids read more, their writing improves.

6

Trivia Quiz

TEST YOUR KNOWLEDGE
ABOUT THE HARRY POTTER BOOKS

1. Who published the Harry Potter Books in the United States?

2. Who published the books in Britain?

3. How many copies have been sold?

4. How many languages have the books been translated into?

5. When was *Harry Potter and the Sorcerer's Stone* published?

6. When was *Harry Potter and the Chamber of Secrets* published?

7. When was *Harry Potter and the Prisoner of Azkaban* published?

8. What place do the Harry Potter books hold on the *New York Times* bestseller list?

9. What is J. K. Rowling's first name? Her nick-name?

10. Name the very first book she wrote, and when she wrote it.

11. What university did J. K. Rowling attend?

12. What was her first career, after she graduated?

13. What was she doing when she got the idea for the Harry Potter books?

14. Where was she when she got it?

15. Where did she begin writing the Harry Potter books?

16. On what did she begin to write it?

17. Who gave her a grant to finish writing the book?

18. How many pages are in the first book?

19. Who illustrated the Harry Potter books?

20. What prizes have the Harry Potter books won?

Trivia Quiz Answers

1. Scholastic, Inc.
2. Bloomsbury Publishing
3. 2 million copies in Britain and over 5 million in the United States
4. 28 languages
5. In Britain, June 1997; in the United States, September 1998
6. In 1998
7. In Britain, July 1999; in the United States, August 1999
8. The top three slots
9. Joanne; Jo
10. *Rabbit*, written when she was six years old
11. Exeter University in Britain
12. Teaching school
13. Writing a novel for adults
14. On a train
15. At a café in Edinburgh, Scotland
16. A napkin
17. The Scottish Arts Council
18. 309 pages
19. Mary Grandpré
20. In Britain, the 1997 National Book Award, the 1997 British Book Awards Children's Book of the Year, and the 1997 Smarties Prize; in the United States, *Publishers Weekly* Best Book of 1998, *School Library Journal* Best Book of 1998, *Parenting* Book of the Year Award 1998, New York Public Library Best Book of the Year 1998, an ALA Notable Book

7

Survey of Our Opinions

Favorite Character: Harry

Second Most Favorite Character: Hermione

Favorite Teacher: Headmaster Albus Dumbledore

Second Most Favorite Teacher: Professor Minerva McGonagall

Favorite Animal: Owl

Second Most Favorite Animal: Hippogriff

Most Hated Character: Professor Severus Snape

Second Most Hated Character: Draco Malfoy

Most Frightening Magical Creature: Dementor

Most Annoying Magical Creature: Peeves the Poltergeist

Most Lovable Magical Creature: Dobby the House Elf

Whether Quidditch Can Be Played on the Ground: There were slightly more children who tried to play it or thought it possible than those who didn't

Favorite Food: Every Flavor Beans

Most Hated Food: Every Flavor Beans

Most Popular Broomstick: Nimbus Two Thousand (Surprise! Not the Firebolt!)

Whether to Call Yourself a Muggle If You're Not a Wizard: Evenly divided between those who say a Muggle is a Muggle, and those who say you don't have to be a Muggle just because you're not a wizard

What the Next Book Should Be About: Quidditch, Quidditch, and Quidditch

8

Word Wizardry

BREAK THE MAGICIAN'S SPELL
AND FIGURE OUT THESE WIZARD WORDS

A mischievous wizard has cast a spell over the following words to keep you from reading them. Use your magic "spelling" wand to turn them back into real and useful words.

1. WARDIZ
2. GIMAC
3. KNIRD
4. OTONIP
5. TYDANIT
6. TOANICE
7. NEEDITONT
8. COSERC
9. DINKEY
10. OIVED
11. LUPPER

12. TRAMPLOF
13. GLEATHUR
14. ARDROILA
15. NARRYBRENC
16. CROSRERE
17. MABBLENOIA
18. RONTEMS
19. LUBELARM
20. TEWESS
21. KISTOMBORC
22. SLEEV
23. ASKUPEALBEN
24. TEBLOST
25. SHTOG
26. CAWSHIND
27. GUDEF
28. ZEPULZ
29. TROCCORINST
30. LOVARF
31. TRIVEOFA
32. SHECS
33. ALCOTOSHEC
34. URNDOG
35. STODA
36. NEPORRIS
37. TELSCA
38. SETRINIM
39. CANCITED
40. SEPARNTNART
41. NISSOSSE
42. LECLODID
43. NEYREG
44. KEPTCO
45. SIBILFEED
46. MORTIROYD

Answers:

1.	WIZARD	33.	CHOCOLATE
2.	MAGIC	34.	GROUND
3.	DRINK	35.	TOADS
4.	POTION	36.	PRISONER
5.	DITTANY	37.	CASTLE
6.	ACONITE	38.	MINISTER
7.	DETENTION	39.	ACCIDENT
8.	SOCCER	40.	TRANSPARENT
9.	KIDNEY	41.	SESSIONS
10.	VIDEO	42.	COLLIDED
11.	PURPLE	43.	ENERGY
12.	PLATFORM	44.	POCKET
13.	LAUGHTER	45.	DISBELIEF
14.	RAILROAD	46.	DORMITORY
15.	CRANBERRY		
16.	SORCERER		
17.	ABOMINABLE		
18.	MONSTER		
19.	UMBRELLA		
20.	SWEETS		
21.	BROOMSTICK		
22.	ELVES		
23.	UNSPEAKABLE		
24.	BOTTLES		
25.	GHOST		
26.	SANDWICH		
27.	FUDGE		
28.	PUZZLE		
29.	CONSTRICTOR		
30.	FLAVOR		
31.	FAVORITE		
32.	CHESS		

9

Wonderful Ways
to Be a Wizard

So you want to become a wizard! Of course, as you know, it isn't easy. As with any art, you must study and practice. You must start at the very beginning with simple exercises and continue building your skills as you learn more.

The first thing you need is a costume. A long black robe is the usual wizard outfit, but many wizards wear colors. The famous Merlin, who was King Arthur's personal wizard, is often shown in pictures wearing a robe covered with astrological symbols, and suns, moons and stars. You could choose different colors to enhance different spells, such as sky blue to help you transport yourself through the air, or red-orange to help you summon a flame.

You'll also need a wizard's hat, a conical cap that comes to a point on top and has a flat brim. The pointed top is said to help deflect spells cast upon the wizard who wears the cap. This kind of hat was first worn in Europe during the Middle Ages (sometimes called the Dark Ages!) by scholars as well as magicians. These wizard's hats are usually black, but that's not absolutely required. Some wizards also cover their hats with signs and symbols and runes.

Next, a wand. Wands are usually made of a flexible wood, like willow twigs, which is easy to wave through the air. The success you have with your wand depends on your own skill. Like most items in a wizard's kit, a wand can't be preprogrammed by another wizard.

Pointy-toed shoes are frequently worn by wizards, but they aren't necessary. Some wizards we know wear sneakers! The points on the toes help extend the distance the wearer's spells can travel.

Now that you're outfitted, you may need to learn a few languages before you can cast spells and read wizard manuals. Latin, Greek and Hebrew are the languages wizards most often use, although a lot of wizard lore is coded by wizards themselves or turned into riddles and anagrams.

Wizards also use symbols and runes. Some spells, especially defensive charms, require the performer to draw these symbols in concentric circles on the ground, then stand in the center of the circles before pronouncing the words of the spell.

Herbs and plants used in wizardry grow all around

us and are used to flavor food, but non-wizards don't know how to use them. Wizards and other kinds of magicians, like shamans and non-medical healers, use them to cure ailments and ease pain, as well as to create potions. You will find books on herbs, where they grow and how to identify them, in any library.

Mixing potions is a special art. As in baking cakes, concocting a magic potion requires measuring ingredients exactly and using no substitutes. Some potions may cause a person to fall asleep, others to make him or her fall in love! Of course, some wizard potions actually taste good. Mulled cider is an example of a delicious potion that everyone enjoys drinking, but only wizards know how to use it for making magic.

Some wizards learn to foretell the future by using astrology, palmistry, gazing into crystal balls or reading tea leaves. Astrologers make maps of the stars as they look from the Earth, at the moment of a person's birth or at the time an event happens. They make their predictions based on their knowledge of the powers held by each planet and star, and the significance of their position to each other.

Palmistry, or palm-reading, is based on the significance of the different lines or wrinkles that appear on a person's hand. A fortune-teller may stare into a crystal ball and see a vision of things to come. To read tea leaves, a wizard examines the bits of tea leaves left in a person's teacup after he or she has drunk up the tea. The wizard notes what objects the bits resemble, and bases his predictions on the symbolism of those objects.

10

What We Think Harry Potter's Parents Were Like

A Summary of Our Theories About Their Occupations, Residences and Relationships

Since Harry never knew his parents, we can't help imagining what they were like, what they did for a living and where they lived. Here are some of our ideas.

Some of us think that Harry's parents weren't exactly killed, but had a really bad spell put on them that can't be broken, unless maybe Harry grows up to be the most powerful wizard ever and frees them from the spell.

Before he died, Harry's father may have been . . .
- A practicing wizard
- A professional Quidditch player

- A commentator for Quidditch games
- Working in the real world and using his wizard powers to make a living, for instance, by affecting the stock market or running a health club
- Living in a house in the Forbidden Forest at Hogwarts

Before she died, Harry's mother may have been . . .
- A practicing wizard
- A housewife who did the chores
- A writer of books about magic
- Living in the real world and helping her husband run a health club or some other business
- Working at an ordinary job, like schoolteacher or nurse, in the Muggle world. Her parents on both sides were Muggles, so she was not as good a wizard as Harry's father.

After Harry's parents had a spell put on him,
they may have . . .
- Lived as a stag and doe in the Forbidden Forest
- Hidden out with their Hogwarts friends, who were under oath not to reveal their whereabouts, even to Harry
- Been protected by the magic powers of Albus Dumbledore
- Floated around in a trance, or in a bubble in outer space or on an astral plane

11

What We'd Like to See in the Future Books About Harry Potter

We want to see how Harry and his friends grow up and what they become, whom they marry, and what kinds of careers they have.

We'd like to see Harry play Quidditch professionally and win the Quidditch World Cup. We want him to get a new broom. We want him to beat the Slytherin team again every year.

Harry should have a girlfriend, maybe Cho Chang, the Ravenclaw Quidditch Seeker. We want Ron to have a girlfriend, too.

We hope that Snape gets the position of Defense Against the Dark Arts Professor, or that Harry overmasters him, or that he comes to like Harry. We hope that Draco Malfoy will get expelled from Hogwarts.

The Dursleys should begin to appreciate Harry, or something bad should happen to them.

We think Harry should go to live with Sirius Black, if not right away then sometime in the future.

There should be some new courses at Hogwarts, and Harry should learn to do some new kinds of magic.

Hagrid ought to be happy, and one way would be to give him back his job as teacher of Care of Magical Animals. Also, Hagrid should get his favorite hippogriff, Buckbeak, back.

We want to see more of Ginny, Ron, Fred and George Weasley, but we think Percy should graduate or go elsewhere.

We want to see what else Hermione learns to do.

There should be a new Defense Against the Dark Arts Professor in every book.

If you love Harry Potter as much as we do,
send us your comments, ideas, letters
to Harry, Hermione, Hagrid and all the others,
or any other thoughts on the whole
Hogwarts crew to:

Department JW, Editorial
St. Martin's Press
175 Fifth Avenue
New York, N.Y. 10010

Remember to include your name, address, and
daytime phone number.